PENGUIN BOOKS

# MOST OF US ARE HERE AGAINST OUR WILL

David Levinson was born in San Antonio, Texas. His work has appeared in *The James White Review*, *The New Penguin Book of Gay Short Stories*, *RE:AL*, and *Newsweek*. This is his first book.

# david levinson

## ~~most of us are here~~
## against our will

PENGUIN BOOKS

PENGUIN BOOKS

Published by the Penguin Group
Penguin Books Ltd, 80 Strand, London WC2R ORL, England
Penguin Group (USA) Inc., 375 Hudson Street, New York, New York 10014, USA
Penguin Group (Canada), 10 Alcorn Avenue, Toronto, Ontario, Canada M4V 3B2
(a division of Pearson Penguin Canada Inc.)
Penguin Ireland, 25 St Stephen's Green, Dublin 2, Ireland
(a division of Penguin Books Ltd)
Penguin Group (Australia), 250 Camberwell Road, Camberwell, Victoria 3124, Australia
(a division of Pearson Australia Group Pty Ltd)
Penguin Books India Pvt Ltd, 11 Community Centre, Panchsheel Park, New Delhi – 110 017, India
Penguin Group (NZ), cnr Airborne and Rosedale Roads, Albany, Auckland 1310, New Zealand
(a division of Pearson New Zealand Ltd)
Penguin Books (South Africa) (Pty) Ltd, 24 Sturdee Avenue, Rosebank 2196, South Africa

Penguin Books Ltd, Registered Offices: 80 Strand, London WC2R ORL, England

www.penguin.com

First published by Viking 2004
Published in Penguin Books 2005
1

Copyright © David Levinson, 2004
All rights reserved

The moral right of the author has been asserted

Set by Rowland Phototypesetting Ltd, Bury St Edmunds, Suffolk
Printed in England by Clays Ltd, St Ives plc

# acknowledgements

I thank the following folks for their ongoing support: Emily Stone, the constable of Court Street; Michael Thomas, the James Baldwin of our age; Rone Shavers and his brain; the film guru, Brian Sloan; Grant Navin; Will Lippincott and Palimpsest; Alexander Chee; David Gates; Jill Ciment; the New School faculty; Mimi Levinson; Jane South; Xavier Smith and Buddha; Junot Diaz way back when; Eileen Max; Scott Blackwood; all my buddies at Packer Collegiate; and my students at the University of Texas.

My editor, Zelda Turner, and publisher, Tony Lacey, and all the Penguins – you've made my first time painless and bright. Thank you.

To Charles, Michael, Jennifer and Zachary Levinson – much love. To my mother, Fran, if you weren't already, I'd have you sainted.

Eileen Cope, one of the best eggs and agents in town.

The Corporation of Yaddo.

Finally, to friends here and gone, you're always with me.

# contents

# jaguar

After Don leaves her at the door with a kiss, Regina makes the bed and tells herself that this is the last time. Though she appreciates his attention, the flowers, candy, trinkets, enough is enough; she knows how things like this end. The framed poster, which Don gave her three weeks ago, leans against her bedroom wall: *Your life is not your own . . . yet*. At the window, she parts the curtains to make sure Don isn't sitting in his car; that he's truly gone. I can't let this go on, Regina thinks, grabbing her pocketbook.

A chilly morning in Austin, the wind revolves in gentle cycles about her, stirring leaves and empty Styrofoam cups. She stands on Spyglass Drive, the spread of squat buildings as unfamiliar as she herself feels. The Rialto Cinema, the abandoned art house, sits across the street like an indecent eruption. Jagged teeth of broken windows, stucco façade discoloured and swollen from rain, acne of black spray paint with silly messages. Regina's favourite: *L. Ron Hubbard lives in my cupboard!* The red-lettered neon sign tilts at an obdurate angle. Sometimes, in the middle of the night, Regina awakens to the flickering letters, which illumine her bedroom like

1

a bordello. And stays up agonizing over what Lucille, her older sister, will do when and if she finds out about Don's amourous persistence.

Rolling up in her Jaguar, Lucille says, 'Here I am,' as Regina climbs into the car. She kisses her sister on the cheek. Lucille has taken time out of her busy morning regimen of yoga, beauty parlour, and massage to chauffeur Regina to pick up the used Saab 900. Regina relishes the idea of not having to rely on the bus or Lucille anymore: a ride to HEB's Central Market for groceries and the Arboretum out on MoPac where she took a job as a salesgirl at Ralph Lauren. It's so great to have a rich sister, she thinks, blowing on her hands, her breath frozen milk.

'Can we make this kind of quick? Don isn't feeling well and we have our housewarming party tonight,' she says. 'You *are* coming, aren't you, Gina?' Lucille's the only person in the world who still calls her Gina. It harks back to their girlhood, lying on each other's beds and taking those silly quizzes in *Seventeen*. 'I invited Stu, a friend of Don's from work. He's dying to meet you,' she adds.

'Lucille, come on,' Regina says. 'I'm not exactly dating material right now.'

She lowers the visor and catches the rough, craggy impression of her face in the mirror. Though she's no longer that same girl who used to watch Lucille kissing Peter in the Rialto, that girl is still there, expectant.

'Nonsense. Just wear something low-cut,' Lucille says, as they pull onto the highway. They pass an old truck with an oblong dent in its side and suddenly Regina longs for bed, for the boxes in her apartment, to sift through them for the person she was in Quito. When she made real decisions that could change lives: redirecting fingers of the river for irrigation, checking the water for ovine bacteria, whether or not to build a footbridge. Choosing what outfit to wear to meet a man she doesn't know seems the height of frivolity to her.

In less than twenty minutes, Lucille brakes in the parking lot of Consolidated Car Outlet. The cars in the lot shimmer, many of them shaped, Regina muses, like the diet pills they wolfed down in college, because, according to Lucille, boys liked to see bones. The traffic skitters by on the highway, breathing past her. She watches the traffic, remembering Carlos and his dusty, sky-blue Chevy, which rattled and broke down every few miles. Damn him and his truck, Regina thinks. She sees his hands again, loose on the steering wheel, the embattled skin, tiny scars from fighting. She loved his fingers, the way they bent and unbent into a secret history meant just for her.

Regina wanders around, listening to Lucille on her cellphone. She hears, 'It doesn't mean anything, Don. Really.' And then, 'No, Don, I told you frangipanis. Frangipanis, Don.'

The moment she leans a foot on the bumper of a Datsun, the man who sold her the Saab rushes out of the office. To her, his untamed moustache still looks like a tarantula fell asleep on his upper lip. The moustache offers him a frontiersman's credibility, as if to say, *You can trust me, little lady*. All he needs now, Regina thinks, is a tin star and a ten-gallon hat.

'The Saab's all ready for you,' he says. 'Washed, dried, and pressed.'

The lives of salesmen, she thinks, and sighs. His face widens into a smile. 'Follow me,' he says, twisting one hairy leg of his grey moustache into a point.

She leaves Lucille shouting at Don about stuffed

mushrooms and follows him through a labyrinth of Volvos, BMWs, Toyotas. She spies her first choice again, a shiny, dark blue Chevy truck, and remembers the story he told her: That it was traded in by a father who lost his only son, a graduation present from college. And with only a few thousand miles – a real bargain. She decided instead on the ten-year-old automatic Saab, foam-green with tan interior. Everything about it ran just this side of smooth, including the squeaking sunroof and crackling stereo.

Finished with Don at last, Lucille pokes her head into the office, smoking. Her long cashmere trench coat billows behind her like an imperial flag. 'Emergency at home,' she says to Regina. 'Call me later.' Then, like the ashes of her cigarette, she blows away.

Regina speeds down Congress to Manuel's, the expensive Mexican restaurant where Lucille told her Peter Benotti has been a *maître d'* for years. She idles in the lot, watching him at the lectern under a dim halo of pink light. He's involved with the phone, speaking animatedly while his fingers scratch at his beard. Thin and fragile, a mix of dark and light, Southern Italian and Swedish, if memory serves her. His hand shakes as he brings the phone up to his lips and Regina's heart does a shimmy in her chest. She remembers how much she liked Peter. The moist plum lips, the delicate bones of his cat-like face, the mop of black hair. The way he said her name, with a tiny punch on the first syllable. And what a smile!

The Saab purrs drowsily and she puts on the head-lights, casting great arcs in the dusk. The rapids of traffic jerk and die, every red light timed with man-made precision. The world is a series of traffic lights, she thinks. So unlike what she'd grown used to in Ecuador, the quiet, empty dirt roads and rustling fields of sorghum. No one rushing. No traffic.

Regina thinks back to the first time she rode in Carlos's truck, the day he drove her back to his house. The catalpa tree in his front yard. The kiss on his porch. They'd met at the payphone outside the barbershop in town, where Carlos was getting his beard trimmed. She pulls into her apartment complex and climbs out. Standing back, she hits the tiny button on her key chain that switches on the burglar alarm. The tail-lights flash three times and the horn bleeps once and then, silence. She touches the car's hood; warm, like a heart. She lays her head on the hood, smoothly.

'I love you,' she says.

Her apartment greets her with an obscene quiet which, after three weeks, she no longer trusts. Soon, the neighbours next door will hurl pots against the paper-thin walls, and send their boy out into the hall. Regina waits in the threshold for these domestic nuisances, the apartment neither cosy nor fetching. She has two hours before Lucille's party and wonders what to do. I could unpack and make this place liveable, she thinks, flinging off her mules, toes cold and brittle.

'Buy appropriate shoes,' she says into the empty, rectangular room, massaging her feet, as the first of the artillery smashes against the wall. She jumps, hears the muffled screams of the wife, a dowdy young woman who baked her an oyster casserole to welcome her to the building. Uneaten, it sits in the refrigerator collecting spores and mould.

Lying down in the middle of the unfurnished room, Regina clutches the keys to her car and thinks of Peter. Through her correspondence with Lucille over the last

5

four years, she heard of Peter's wife's suicide, and the subsequent loss of his job at the university. *As you know, since you dated him, he was never much of a drinker*, Lucille wrote, *but Gina, I swear to God that's all he did for six months! Once, he even showed up at my office at Huggins' Realty blitzed out of his gourd!* Though she found this revision of the facts amusing, she didn't bother reminding Lucille that it was she who'd dated him, not her.

Bad things always happen to the wrong people, Regina thinks, staring up at the silver-speckled ceiling, which reminds her of the stars above Carlos's roof. The ceiling sold her on the apartment. That and how inexpensive it was. She rises off the linoleum and goes to the telephone. She dials 411, gets the number of Manuel's. She asks for Peter Benotti, and is told to hold. A soft instrumental – music she abhors because, without words, what's the point? – drifts out of the receiver. Regina hangs on the line and, about to give up, he says, 'Peter speaking. May I make a reservation for you?'

Regina wants to hang up. Suddenly, she feels foolish calling Peter, Lucille's old boyfriend. She can't believe the way her culture shock is manifesting itself, making her do these crazy things. She says, softly, 'Peter, it's Regina Coombs, from high school.'

'Oh, hey, Regina,' Peter says, reserved in the way of *maître d*'s everywhere. 'Didn't I just see you? That was you, right, in the Saab?'

Regina smiles. 'Yes, guilty,' she says.

'Regina Coombs,' Peter says, as if trying to remember someone else. 'Weren't you in Guatemala?'

'Ecuador,' she says. 'But I'm back now.'

'I actually thought you were Lucille,' he says, his voice

adrift in what, Regina assumes, is memory. 'Did you want to make a reservation?'

Regina breathes in. 'No. I mean, do you have any plans tonight? I'm supposed to go to this party and I don't really want to and I thought it would be fun if you were there,' she says. 'The catch is – because there's always a catch right? – it's at Lucille's.' A heavy sigh. 'Peter?'

He hangs up.

Regina holds the phone away from her, as the second round of pots smash against the wall.

Already running an hour late, Regina finds the entrance to MoPac, the highway that will take her to her sister's house. Snow, a confusing sight here in the Capital City of Texas, doubly confuses her and has thrown Austin into pandemonium. Though barely an inch has accumulated on the ground, men in giant yellow trucks scatter sawdust and salt from buckets anyway. 'Will you look at that?' says the disc jockey. 'If y'all didn't believe it before, you gotta believe it now: it's the seventh sign.' In the background, Michael Stipe croons, 'It's the end of the world as we know it and I feel fine.'

Passing Zilker Park, where 'South-by-Southwest', the great music festival happens, and the convention centre, the one everyone hates, which looks like an alien space-craft, Regina somehow winds up on Highway 35 going south, toward San Antonio. She knows this is wrong, since Lucille told her they moved north of the city, into the hills. Regina pulls over to search for the directions, but having left the apartment in a flurry of forgetfulness, she can't find them. Nine o'clock speeds away, and by the time she reaches a payphone, a terrible cry comes from under the Saab's hood.

She shuts off the engine and sits there, while the snow dusts the windshield. She gives it a good five minutes and then pumps the gas and turns the key in the ignition. Nothing. The car stays quiet, the gauges dark. She sighs. Regina knows a thing or two about cars from Carlos, but not nearly enough, she thinks, dialing the Huggins's. Don answers. In the background, Regina hears the doorbell chime and voices rise.

'Hi,' she says, 'it's Regina.'

'Regina,' he says, 'what gives? You're late.'

'I'm lost,' she says. 'I thought I could find your new place without directions. I was wrong, I guess.'

'Where are you?' Don says.

Regina looks at the street signs. 'Nowhere near you. Did they change the direction of the highways or something while I was gone?' Don chuckles. 'I'm at an Amoco station, in San Marcos,' she says. 'Far?'

Don chuckles again. 'San Marcos?' he says. 'How the heck did you wind up there?'

'The car led me,' she says. 'I had nothing to do with it.'

'Ah, yes, the blame-the-old-car routine,' he says. 'Well, you have to get back on 35 and . . .'

'The car, it won't start,' Regina says, ashamed, fumbling in her purse. She looks for her wallet and realizes she's misplaced that as well. 'Shit,' she mumbles.

'What? What is it?' he says.

'I forgot my wallet,' she says.

'Call a cab,' he says. 'I'll pay for it when you get here. And Regina, we'll take care of the car tomorrow. What'd you get anyway?'

'A 1991 Saab,' she says proudly. 'Only one hundred and forty thousand miles on it, too.'

'You bought a ten-year-old car?' he says, annoyed.

'Lucille told me to get whatever made me happy,' Regina says, a child scolded unfairly because she simply followed the rules. If people would only say what they really meant, she thinks. She wonders if there isn't something else going on beyond the fraying of his nerves brought on by throwing a party, beyond the constant deflection of his advances towards her.

'Let's talk about it later,' Don says.

'Fine,' Regina says.

A waiter in a starched white shirt with a lopsided grin holds out a tray of shrivelled, oily canapés. Regina takes one, feeling a clutter in her throat. A thought: borrowing money from Don and Lucille was a terrible mistake. She swallows the thought down, along with the canapé, and takes another.

Lucille greets her in a simple black dress, a choker of dark pearls fastened at her throat. She's a stunning display of thin, aerobicized arms and narrow waist. The crêpe de Chine falls down her body in perfect lines, accenting the fullness of her chest. Regina hasn't seen her in a dress in years. And it's impossible for her to tell which of her breasts is real and which one the prosthesis.

'I'm sorry I didn't bring a bottle of anything,' Regina says at the upstairs window of the guest bedroom.

'Oh, don't worry about that,' Lucille says. 'We're being catered.'

Below them, the house fills with more and more guests, women in furs, men in dark blue suits. Regina spots them on the sidewalk. Everyone tan and happy, at least from the sounds of their voices. Soft ships of snow drop past the window onto the expanse of yard. She wants to go outside and make angels, build a snowman, start a snowball fight.

9

'I saw Peter Benotti today,' Regina says. 'You remember him.'

'Peter Benotti,' Lucille repeats, fixing a loose curl of hair.

Regina sighs. 'You dated him in college, Lucille,' she says.

'I did?' she says.

Don comes into the room wielding a bouquet of long-stemmed peach-coloured roses. 'Where do I put these?' he says.

'They're gorgeous,' Lucille says. 'Who from?'

'Stu,' Don says. 'He just arrived.' He turns to Regina and says, 'He's waiting downstairs for you.' His voice isn't cold, as Regina expected, only keen, like a blade. Regina imagines he uses this voice at work at the bank, where he's vice-president. Uses it in bed with Lucille. It is a commanding voice, of armies and women. And someone like Don, attractive, with the bone structure and colouring of Vikings, can get away with it. Guys like Don have always gotten away with it, Regina thinks.

The three descend the stairs together and then she is part of the drink-toting, cigarette-smoking mob. She watches Lucille and Don disappear with the roses around the corner. The doorbell rings. While Regina waits for someone to answer it, she catches the sound of Lucille's voice, loud and fretful, and then a crash in the kitchen. The doorbell rings again. Regina opens the door and there is Peter, standing with hands behind his back.

'What are you doing here?' she says. 'I thought you were holding a grudge.'

'I am, but, well, I can hold it and be here too. I can do two things at once,' he says.

He shuffles inside, keeping his hands behind his back.

Regina smells the residue of smoke coming off him in delicious waves.

'These are for you,' he says and hands over a bouquet of multicoloured wild flowers, shabby from the cold, their faces withered.

'Thanks, Peter,' she says, taking the flowers.

Peter enters the house, shucks off his ratty overcoat dusted with flecks of melting snow.

'Aren't you freezing in that thing?' Regina says.

'It gets me through,' Peter says. Sadness barrels through her. She thinks again of his wife, the suicide. Behind the smoke, she sees the tenable traces of grief. Having settled, the bones of his face seem anachronistic, like some study by the Flemish Masters. She wants to reach out a hand to stroke his cheek.

'Mind if I interrupt?' It's Don, handsome Don, with another man, nearly the same height and weight. 'Regina, this is Stu.' He pauses, stares vacantly at Peter. 'We haven't met. I'm Don Huggins.'

'Peter Benotti,' he says, extending his hand. 'I'm an old friend of Regina's here. I hope it's okay that I showed up. I mean, I wasn't actually invited.'

'Fine, fine. Not a problem,' Don says. 'Any friend of Regina's . . .'

'We all went to high school together,' Regina says. 'Me, Lucille, and Peter.'

'That's right,' Lucille says, stepping into their circle. 'Peter, it's really great to see you again.'

Champagne is opened and poured and the room erupts into music and dissonance. Regina drinks. She loves the taste of bubbles in her mouth, the way they break apart. She dances with Stu, an affable, charming enough man, the sway of the music in her ears. She loses Peter and Lucille. She forgets where she is. She forgets

11

about Carlos, her once young and sexy lover. She forgets she ever left home for the jungle, for a dot on a map she could barely pronounce. Where she was that American girl or 'the girl with red hair', one of Carlos's endearments.

At one point, Stu says, 'Thanks for the dance,' and goes to smoke.

Don appears magically in his place, as if he's been there all along. 'Still the life of the party, huh?' he says.

'You're confusing me with someone else,' Regina says.

'I don't think so,' he says. 'I know all about you, Regina. Remember: I'm Lucille's husband.'

'Then Lucille must've been talking about herself,' she says.

Don blows a warm, stale stream across her face and says, 'You know I don't really care about the car. I'll buy you another if that one doesn't run.'

'Thanks, Don,' Regina says and as the music becomes a ballad, his hand finds her shoulder.

They dance slowly, Regina keeping her body bowed so as not to touch his. She knows where this can lead. Even if Don weren't Lucille's husband, she thinks, I'm not sure anything would be different. Still, when Don pulls her into him, she feels the tiniest wilting joy at letting go. She hasn't felt this sort of warmth in a while, and now, she's intoxicated on it, the champagne, the smell of Don, his sweat and aftershave. She draws him away from the music to a tenebrous corner, hidden from view by a curio cabinet, and there, she kisses him. In that second, when their lips join, when she tastes the full extent of Don's drunkenness, she misses Carlos more than ever. And recalls, with a stultifying pain, the evening she paid him an unannounced visit.

When she got to his house, Carlos's truck was parked

outside as usual. The sun had already set. The wind ran through the streets kicking up dust. She heard him in the house, his voice loud and resonant, so unlike the voice she was used to. It terrified and excited her. Stepping quietly to the window, she pressed an ear against the glass. She heard the sound of the bed squeaking, heard a woman's laughter, *I love you's* flowing from her mouth, American as hers. Betrayal didn't boil up in Regina, but the disappointing clarity of where she'd always been.

Three months later, on the plane, she wondered how she'd been able to do it. To suspend herself above her life for that long, as if she were a trapeze artist balancing the skinny rope. Holding back a lifetime of regrets, what-ifs, should-have-been's. And how, without warning, the rope unravelled and as she tumbled, she remembered: Oh yes, this is what unhappiness feels like.

Still falling as the kiss ends, Regina pulls away, less ashamed than mystified, and sees Lucille rushing from the room. My God, she thinks, the contents of her stomach curdling. Don slumps down to the floor, head against the wall, and closes his eyes. Regina rushes upstairs to the bathroom, and shuts the door. She throws open the window and sucks down the frigid night air. It clears the images of Carlos from her, two years with a man already married.

Below her, she hears screams, which subside into crackles of laughter. A couple, drunk and in love, tear through the yard, quacking. The woman, in her high heels and mink stole, pins the man, many years her junior, against the snow-dusted hood of a parked car. The quacks become howls. Mating calls, Regina thinks, while particles of ice pelt the screen. Regina shuts the window.

She sits on the toilet, flips through *Cosmo*. She learns

about the price of weddings, how to find her partner's erogenous zones, tubal ligations, ectopic pregnancies. Things she never thought about in Ecuador because there were other things to occupy her: droughts, cholera, dysentery. Raging storms that threatened livestock, lives. Where have I been? she wonders, closing the magazine. And how do I get back there?

Regina descends the stairs to find Peter hovering over a prostrate Don, whose nose is bleeding. The last guests trail smoke out the door and then it is simply the three of them. 'What happened?' she says. 'Where's Lucille?'

'He called you a whore,' Peter says, 'so I decked him.'

'Peter,' Regina says, staring at Don. 'Savage,' she says.

'What should I do?' Peter says.

'I don't know. How about stick him in a pot, boil him and eat him?' she says. 'I mean, what is wrong with you?'

She calls out Lucille's name. Nothing. She goes outside, walks the perimeter of the house. No sign of Lucille anywhere. Then, Regina hears music coming from the garage. And there is Lucille sitting in the Jaguar.

'Go away,' she says as Regina climbs in beside her, the plush leather seat turning her drowsiness into fatigue. She shuts her eyes and imagines living inside the Jaguar, this sleek relic of chrome and wood and steel.

'I will not,' Regina says over the music. 'I'm here to stay.'

'Why'd you come back?' her sister says. 'To torture me again like when we were girls?'

'I told you why,' she says. 'It was time to go. And who tortured who, Lucille?'

'You kissed my husband, Gina,' Lucille says, placing her hands on the steering wheel. Ten and two o'clock, just how they'd been taught.

'It was an accident,' she says.

'There are no accidents,' Lucille says, starting the car. 'I'm taking you home.'

They glide to the edge of the driveway. 'What about Peter?' Regina says.

'He broke Don's nose,' Lucille says. 'Let him find his own way home.'

'Lucille, please,' Regina says, opening her door. 'You know Don probably deserved it.'

She runs into the house, grabs a bottle of Veuve Cliquot from the fridge, and ushers Peter out the door. They drive in silence through the snowy Austin streets and enter a run-down neighbourhood, with plain, squat houses and postage stamp-size yards. Chain link fences instead of privet hedges.

'That one, right there,' Peter says.

Lucille pulls up to a modest one-storey house, red brick façade, white trim. The dark windows cast no reflection. It is the sort of house, Regina imagines, which contains brown shag carpet, a cigarette-scarred La-Z-Boy recliner, yellowed linoleum streaked and scuffed with neglect. She wonders if Peter has always lived here, if this is all he can afford.

'This is me,' he says. 'We'll have to hang out again real soon.' Regina feels a wild desperation to explain the facts: she meant the kiss for a different man. But Peter bounds away before she has a chance.

In the rearview mirror, she watches Lucille gazing at him. Regina adds, 'Don's been sending me flowers and candy, Lucille. I thought you ought to know, that's all.'

'Oh, great,' Lucille says, her voice small, breakable.

'So you thought you'd reward him with a kiss? Gina, we weren't raised to be sluts.'

Regina lets this hang between them. She allows Lucille her sadness, the knowledge that when she gets home, she'll meet her husband with a new set of eyes.

As Lucille pulls away from Peter's, Regina says, 'You're right. I am a slut.' She pauses. 'In Ecuador, I fell in love with a married man. And I couldn't bear to be in the same country with him so I left.' Lucille accelerates, and the tyres disengage the road. They slide to an abrupt stop against the curb, unharmed. 'But do you know why I left Austin?' Lucille shakes her head. 'Because I wasn't about to lose my own life to help you win yours back.'

And just like that, they become two strangers in a car on a freakish, snowy night. 'I was wretched to you, Lucille,' Regina says. 'I hate myself because of you.'

Lucille steps out of the car with the bottle of champagne. The headlights catch her and for an instant, it looks as if she's forgotten where she is. She turns her body and cants her hip, a holding pattern of flat back, drooped shoulders and screws of hair. Then, bottle clenched between her thighs, she savages the aluminum foil and the cork, which zings up and away. She brings the bottle to her crinkled lips, and drinks deeply.

Back in the car, Lucille says, 'You never wanted to be you and you hated me for it,' and the taut line of her voice scares Regina, who knows she should get out of the car before it starts moving again, before the doors lock automatically. But the buttery leather of the seat persuades her otherwise. Still, she clutches her hands in her lap, like she did on the way to school, after a morning of cutting up Lucille's bras. After staring at herself in the mirror and asking why she couldn't look more like her sister. She thinks back to those mornings, when they were just girls, when cutting up a bra or borrowing a cashmere sweater without asking was the most terrible thing in the world.

'Don't,' Regina says.

'It's not my fault, Gina,' Lucille says, driving with alacrity. 'When are you going to stop blaming me for –'

'Don't,' Regina says, louder this time.

She's trembling, and she wants out. She scratches at the window, at the door, all the buttons and knobs on the dashboard. The sunroof opens and the snow streaks in, catching in Lucille's once-irradiated, still thin hair. She drives, her face humourless and resigned, as if she's made of something else, something different from Regina.

'– for being who I am. I'm your sister and I love you but I'm not the reason you are the way you are. I really thought after four years you would've gotten on with it. We aren't kids anymore, Gina. You've got to stop lying to yourself. You'll meet someone, I know you will, but making up these wild stories about Don sending you flowers and candy, I mean, really, Gina, who are you kidding? Don's my husband. He's seen me through two miscarriages and a mastectomy. Where were you? I'll tell you: off in some foreign country fucking a married man, while I sat in that hospital room, alone.'

'Let me out of here,' Regina says. 'Stop.'

They are no longer in Austin, but in some remote and hostile place. Regina can't defend herself out here against Lucille, this Lucille, who will go home to Don later that evening and slide into bed beside him, as if nothing at all has happened. Regina knows this just as surely as she now knows that she's losing her resolve for compassion. And without warning, the seed covering of her pity cracks, and Regina says, '"Being with her is like being with a cadaver." ' That's what he said this morning, Lucille. He said a woman like you isn't a woman at all. I have breasts, Lucille. See.'

Regina shrugs off her coat, and slips both straps of her dress down to reveal a pink satin bra. She unclasps the hook to loose her breasts, which hang there, tan and freckled, with a few soft blond hairs circling the areolas. Her nipples harden immediately in the cold. Lucille steers the Jaguar off the highway, her knuckles white on the wheel. While this Regina, this wilderness of a woman, takes a gulp of champagne and says, 'Look, Lucille. This is what Don wants. This is what all men want.'

'It doesn't matter,' Lucille says, sadly, 'because even with Don, you'll always be who you are, Gina: my ugly little sister.'

They pull into the Sandpiper Apartments and the Jaguar comes to rest in the space where the Saab ought to be. Regina shakes as she pulls on her dress, frazzled by her behaviour. The latch to her door pops up and she hurries out with the bottle, slipping on a patch of ice. Knees painful and bloodied, she rises and stares through the windshield. Lucille's face, lit up by the overhead light, smiles contemptuously. So this is who we've become, she thinks, brandishing the bottle above her head, as if it is a club. She brings it down quickly and harshly across the windshield, across the face of her sister who peers out at her with wide, aggrieved eyes. There's beauty in the attempt, grace in the motion. But, to Regina's surprise, as the windshield cracks and the bottle splits like a blister, there's nothing like relief.

As she lopes away, fingers numb, Regina thinks about one of the quizzes Lucille forced her to take as a girl. There was this question: *If you could change one thing*

*about you, what would it be?* As Lucille drives off and
Regina climbs the stairs that lead to her apartment, she
recalls answering that she'd change the colour of her
eyes from mud brown to jungle green, the same shade as
her sister's. What she didn't tell Lucille, because how do
you ever tell someone the truth?, was that she'd give
anything to be an only child. Not just this, to be the
child who survived the car accident, the drowning, the
fire. And in praying for her sister's death, Regina became
its agent. A week after Lucille got cancer, Regina fled to
Ecuador.

Out in the cold hallway, the neighbours' voices
reverberate, tinny and threatening. Comic books and a
glow-in-the-dark water gun lay next to their sleeping
boy. His toes, visible and blue, protrude out of the
sleeping bag, the nails in need of a trim. Regina can
almost see the breath leave his body. She kneels beside
him and shakes his little shoulder. Six or seven years old
at the most, the boy opens his eyes, and yawns.

Regina raises the thermostat in her apartment, the
apartment Lucille found for her, and the warm air
circulates through the vents. She swallows a couple of
aspirin. From the fridge, she pulls the oyster casserole
and dumps it in the trash. Taking down a box of
chocolates, she bites into a caramel. In the morning,
she'll hand over the casserole dish and the boy and the
rest of Don's chocolates to her neighbour. Until then,
there is still getting through the snow and the night and
the boxes of her life.

# the cheerleader's kiss

I didn't notice Mia right away and it was her scent, some flowery attar she wore on special occasions, which stopped me on the page. She always knew where to find me, since I spent most of my free time in the kitchen, at that pickled-pine table. We'd fucked, blended a thousand margaritas, and killed hundreds of plants on that table. Out the window, the imperceptible shift of the neighbour's curtains and the squawk of car alarms, the minutiae of life on the Upper West Side. Decibels, frequencies and my heart, everything rose in an eerie pitch that morning. Mia finally broke through it all, saying, 'It's only temporary, Jed,' and drew a red curl behind her ear.

'Happy endings are temporary,' I said, staring past her to the typewriter, my mug of tepid coffee. 'Divorce isn't, Mia.'

'Did I say *divorce*?' she said. 'I said *separation*. And to use one of your own metaphors: the script of our marriage needs a rewrite. You, Jed, need a rewrite.' She paused. 'You're an unfulfilled man.'

'This is your reason?' I said, with condescension. 'I'm

plenty fulfilled. I have you, this apartment, my screen-play and –'

'Jed, please . . .'

The kitchen went brilliant white as the sun leaped from behind a cloud. The sunlight on Mia's face, a face I'd grown as accustomed to as my own. She wet her cruel lips: red without lipstick, stung-swollen, puckered. I'd married a beautiful girl in Mia, my wife, who taught Art Appreciation at a private school in Brooklyn Heights. Did her students know how fortunate they were? No one had lips like hers.

'I miss Jed Flicker,' she said. 'Where did you put him?'

I made a useless move toward her. Mia flinched, took a step back and then out of the kitchen. She stood with hips canted, her hands lying flat across her chest and in that moment, I knew.

'Where did you put him?' she repeated, softer.

Then, she walked to the front door, gathered her keys from the sideboard, and paused, as if to judge the last few minutes of our marriage all over again.

I reached for a knife, running my finger along the dull blade. It needed sharpening, and so I got out the pumice and oil. When the door opened and shut and I heard Mia's heels in the hallway, I said, 'In the box, with Manfred Stark.'

Mia moved out a week later, snatching the pink velvet love-seat, which we'd had sex on our first night in the apartment.

'High sentimental value,' she'd said as the movers hauled it away.

It had occupied the easternmost corner of the living room and without it the place seemed less habitable, colder. I thought of replacing it with a recliner, but every time I went shopping, I thought only of love-seats. As I had done a few afternoons later, going from one used-furniture store to another with Carter, my best friend.

Now, we sat on the floor in the empty living room, watching MTV. Carter was smoking and I handed him an ashtray.

'Styling and profiling,' he said, checking out the white Playboy bunny stencilled in the bottom. Just another ashtray I'd amassed over the years.

'Mia hates it,' I said.

'I see,' Carter said. 'Well, if you ever want to get rid of it, let me know. It's bound to be worth something one day.'

Mia and I had gone to Las Vegas many years ago. I'd stolen the ashtray from the Mirage. That was when I was smoking two packs of Reds a day. The ashtray was only worth something to me; a souvenir of a more promising time. When we'd snuggle on the love-seat, the sun setting over the park, share a cigarette and one of those cheap bottles of Chianti wrapped in wicker. Mia would cup the ashtray in her slim hand threateningly, the bluish smoke crowning her black hair. 'Don't piss me off,' she'd say, smiling, 'or the ashtray's a goner.' I missed her, the smoke, her wine-red lips.

I opened the window. One of Mia's rules: if you smoke, crack the window. Habits, they're what kept me going. The early-morning sex, the runs in the park, the falafel sandwiches from Fatoosh, our favourite Middle-Eastern dive on Broadway. Something forgettable, like cracking the window.

'So I'll make you an extra set of keys,' I said to Carter.

'Jed, are you sure about this?' he said. 'You hear all sorts of stories about friends who end up despising each other.'

We'd talked that afternoon about Carter staying with me, while Hank, his partner of five years, renovated their apartment. Apparently, it was only going to take him a couple of months. I wanted to help Carter. Where else could he stay free if not with me? (I'd inherited a little money from my father's estate.) I wasn't sure I could live with Carter, but I wasn't sure I couldn't live with him either.

Carter got up and went to the window, clutching the ashtray. 'One-oh-seven and Central Park West,' he said. 'I guess it might be nice to live nearer the park and all. I've just gotten so used to where I am and then of course there's Hank and the apartment . . .' His voice dropped away, and there was real sadness in it.

I knew Carter loved Hank, and that because of this, he refused to see what I did. The shifting glances at other men whenever we went out to dinner, the casual flirtations with the waiters, the mean-spirited cracks about Carter's physical appearance, the musculature lost, the firm, flat stomach ballooning. If any of this bothered him, he never said. It annoyed me.

'I'm sure Hank'll survive without you for a while,' I said.

'That's what I'm afraid of,' he said.

'It's not permanent,' I said, switching off the TV. 'I'll even let you have the bed.'

Carter stubbed out his cigarette, and sighed. 'Jesus, I hate sleeping alone,' he said.

The first couple of weeks were disorienting with Carter in the double bed. I'd find myself tucked up against him by accident, and, more amused than horrified, pull away. Or I'd awaken to Carter's scruffy face against my back, and shift my body around. Over the course of our extended friendship, I'd seen his body turn hairy and muscled, the lines of his face sharpen. I was there when his voice dropped an octave, when he got his driver's licence, when his mom died. I'd seen him through a bout of glandular fever. We'd even made out once, in junior high, pretending to be each other's girlfriends; I'd ended up getting sick too.

That afternoon, I went for a run in the park. Looping around the reservoir, I thought of the reading that night for my screenplay, *Awful Kisses*. I'd been working on the script for eight years.

In the months prior to the reading, I'd sent out dozens of invites to well-known producers, at Miramax, Universal and Paramount. All RSVP'd that yes, they'd attend. Though my two lead actors bowed out at the last minute, I felt secure about Carter, who'd been in a number of independent films. Less so of Mia, though she'd seen the script through multiple drafts. Truth was, my reasons for asking her were selfish; I had to see her again. There were things I hadn't said, things I desperately needed to.

At the rented theatre space on 42$^{nd}$ Street and Twelfth Avenue, I placed all of the actors, except Carter who hadn't yet arrived, in their assigned seats. Each seat held a bottle of Evian, and a note from me thanking the actor personally. Mia shifted uneasily as she read her note: *A glass of Chianti after?* She glanced up and away, past me to the door where the crowd of our friends and my colleagues were smoking and shaking hands. At seven-thirty, Carter was still not among them.

At eight o'clock, I called the last of the smokers inside. They took their seats, some faces familiar, others not. A man with a narrow face kept lifting heavy, black curls from his blue eyes, and from this gesture I knew him.

I'd only met Manfred Stark twice: once, eight years ago at a reading in the East Village and, more recently, on the red-eye from Los Angeles to New York. I was anguished sitting next to him. How could I not be? I'd been transforming one of his stories into a script for years, without his knowledge. It would've been so easy to locate him – there couldn't have been many Manfred Starks in the city – to ask permission. Yet, as the plane descended into Queens, I'd understood I never would. He'd been quite cordial, if not aloof, going so far as to offer me his PO Box – he didn't have a phone, or so he said – so that we might get together for coffee *somewhere sometime*. Aloof, like I'd said.

I hadn't invited him that night and his appearance cast a thorough pall over me.

'Thank you all for coming,' I said. 'In case you're here under duress,' pausing to allow for laughter, 'this is the reading of Jed Flicker's screenplay, *Awful Kisses*.' A couple of hmm's from the front row, which held the producers and directors. Stalling for Carter, I said, 'I'd like to introduce the players now.'

Without him, the reading was bound to fall apart. Not merely because he knew every line by heart, but because he *was* Gus Snyder, the story's anti-hero. From germination to final product, I'd intermittently pictured Carter in the role. No one else could play him with that much complexity, pathos and contempt. I certainly couldn't do it.

When I got to Mia, I pivoted around and said, 'And last but not least, my beautiful wife, Mia, who'll be reading the role of Kate Johnson.'

It was then that Carter hurried through the door in a

flutter of papers and apologies. He slumped down in his seat, his face smudged and eyes red-rimmed. From the looks of him, he'd been crying. 'And this man, who rounds out our cast, is the exceptionally late Carter Gilford,' I said, trying for levity, which failed.

Carter lifted his head, eyes watering, and clapped. Then, he fanned his face and said, 'On with the show.'

During the first act, Carter gave what I can only assume was his best, but what I have to call a mezzanine performance. From high above, someone in the audience might not have noticed the missed cues, the bumbling, understated lines (although the script lay open in his lap), the faulty bravado running through his voice. But we were in a tiny theatre, with about fifty seats, no mezzanine, no balcony. It was as if Carter had never seen the script, never practised repeatedly, had forgotten every rehearsal. It was shaming.

Outside, while everyone smoked and chattered, while Mia moved lushly across the street to the deli to fetch more water, and Stark glided down the block, I said to Carter, 'Are you trying to get back at me for some reason?'

Lifting his eyes to mine, he said, 'You may think the solar system revolves around you, Jed Flicker, but news flash: you're an iota, a speckle. Like the rest of us.'

'Where were you before coming here?' I said, a paternal blandishment in my voice I barely recognized.

He said, 'At La Belle Vie,' the dive bar in Hell's Kitchen, where Carter worked, where the three of us used to hang out. 'Then at Hank's. We were coming here together.' Carter's febrile blue eyes danced back and forth, as if looking for him.

Then, I knew, as I'd always known. 'That sonovabitch,' I said.

'Moving in with you wasn't smart,' he said.

'Hey, now, I was only doing you a favour,' I said. 'Don't go blaming the help because your boyfriend can't keep it in his Jockey's.'

'I'm not going back in there,' he said.

'Carter, let's focus one minute on the future,' I said. 'If you continue to screw this up, and that's just what you're doing, not only won't I get the backing I need, your arse is out on the street. So make a decision: either hit the high notes or live in the park with the rest of the degenerates.'

'Keep it up,' Carter said, 'and you can find yourself another roommate and best friend.'

'Why? You're doing such a spectacular job,' I said, laughing meanly, and left him there to slide in beside Mia who sped into the theatre and took her seat.

To Carter's credit and my utter humility, the second act unfolded without flaws. Every actor, including Mia (the most amateurish of the bunch), had near-perfect timing. Laughs and gasps erupted from the audience on cue. My script crowed with life. Afterward, due plaudits, card-swapping and 'I'll be in touch' from everybody's lips.

Mia hurried away, feigning a 'previous engagement', which left only Carter, there on the stage, hands folded in his lap. How could I have possibly said such horrible things to him?

'You were smashing, old chum,' I said, moving behind him to place my hands on his shoulders. 'Simply smashing.'

'Go to hell, Jed,' he said, shaking me off. Then, he gathered up his belongings and disappeared from the stage.

*

Carter didn't sleep with me that night. Instead, he slept on the floor in the living room, the soft plangent sounds of the TV filtering under my bedroom door. By morning, I figured his mood would've passed, as it did when we were kids. But when I awoke around ten, feeling rested and ready to face him, Carter was already gone.

I went into the kitchen, halved an apple with one of the newly sharpened knives. Then, I sat down to work on the script. I reread my treatment for the producers, a sort of fast-paced snapshot:

> A beleaguered assistant at Paramount, Gus Snyder accidentally comes across an old, never-made script by William Faulkner in one of the studio's archive rooms. He updates it, changing the names, locations, title. The movie, Undertow, gets made to mild critical success. A real sleeper. Years, and many subsequent films later, Gus marries Kate Johnson, his ex-boss's daughter. Rich and famous, the Snyders move into the Hollywood Hills, high above the swamp of Los Angeles.
>
> One day, an article appears in the LA Times about Gus, who, it claims, filched one of William Faulkner's scripts. Gus, under pressure and fearing retaliation, flees Hollywood, leaving Kate and his life behind. He takes a job teaching high school English in New Braunfels, a remote Texas town. He changes his name, cuts his hair, gains weight, all to no avail: he's seduced by one of his students, a beautiful young cheerleader, who recognizes him.
>
> One night, she invites Gus over for dinner, where her mother and father offer their daughter in exchange for his screen-writing abilities, blackmailing him not only into helping them write their own screenplay, but also into getting it made.

I felt a kinship with Gus, perhaps because he too was a failing (and failed) screenwriter, because he too was involved in a relationship going awry. The eerie degrees separating any two people.

Cutting bits of flabby dialogue out of the first act and cleaning up some stage directions in the second, I improved the pace. By noon, the script was a whole five pages lighter and, at ninety-six taut sheets, a perfect length. I rose from the unsteady kitchen table, which Mia and I had picked out together at ABC Home Furnishings. Pickled-pine, it held the faintest of scratches in its grain; already damaged before we'd brought it home. Mia had haggled with the salesman and by the time I knew what was happening, the table was ours. Or mine really: she'd bequeathed it to me.

'Now you have a place to write your beautiful, award-winning screenplays,' she'd said, kissing me in the taxi on the way home.

But I hadn't. Not in eight years. As I headed to 84th and Broadway to see a movie, many movies, I wondered what sort of life awaited *Awful Kisses*. Would it wind up on a shelf, forever unread? Or would it find the right studio, producer, director? I hadn't finished my PhD in Hermeneutics, hadn't ever held a full-time job, and, at thirty-seven years old, had no discernible skills. The résumé of my life was a sham. The only thing I knew how to do was sit at that rickety, scratched-up kitchen table, sip my coffee, and blow smoke.

Around eleven o'clock, I slipped back into the apartment. I'd sat through four bad movies, back to back. Something only someone without any obligations could do. The pith of my stomach ached from all the popcorn and Coke, my eyes like buttons loosely sewn onto my face. I placed my keys in the ceramic bowl and heard stirring in the living room. The strike of a match, Mia's 'Sure', and Carter's giddy laugh, then the silence of smoke. They were drinking, the ice clacking in their glasses like coins. I assumed they'd been at it for a while, the room thick with smoke and whiskey.

Disgusted at myself, at the wasted hours in the dark, I strode to the window and cracked it. The smoke and laughter slowly leached away. I turned my attention behind me to the far corner, where the love-seat had sat those eight long years. I jumped, which brought about more snorts from Mia and Carter.

'Isn't it ridiculous?' Carter said, froths of smoke running off his lips.

Through the chiaroscuro of the room, I saw the statue: a man fashioned out of hollow cathode tubes, rusty syringes, filaments from the inside of a TV, radio transistors, shells from a shotgun, everything encased in a fine layer of beeswax. He was stooped over, eyes cast down, his fingers reaching for a flower, a pinwheel. A semi-famous sculptor, Hank collected these parts from all over the city.

'What is it?' I said.

Carter held up a watery blue square of vellum and read, ' "To my dearest Carter. Something to remember me by. Yours, Hank." It came this afternoon wrapped in brown paper. The bastard actually had it delivered. Luckily, I was at the bar.'

'What is it?' I repeated.

'It's me,' Carter said. 'I've been immortalized.'

'I sort of like it,' Mia said, turning her face toward me. 'Don't you, Jed?'

'Frankly, it gives me the creeps,' I said.

For a moment, I thought about breaking every one of

its joints and tossing it out the window. I know I could've talked Mia into helping me. She always said she disliked Hank and his work as much as I did. Could I really assume what she liked and disliked anymore?

Mia followed me into the kitchen. In the palm of her open hand, she held the thin ashtray with its half-smoked butts. It gave off a deep, dank residue of tar and ash. 'What am I going to do about this?' she said, eyes on the ashtray, her bottom lip imperceptibly swollen and shaded a dark plum. 'I can't bear being without you, Jed, but I can't be with you anymore either.'

'Mia,' I said.

'I keep thinking what Kate would do,' she said. 'But I'm not Kate and you aren't Gus, I guess.'

'Manfred Stark was at the reading,' I said. 'Scrawny, shaggy black hair, livid blue eyes. Remember? He was sitting in the last row.' I paused. 'Did you invite him?'

'Jed,' she sighed.

'So you didn't,' I said, resigned.

Mia shook her head, the long round ash of her cigarette breaking off and falling on her shoe.

'Here, let me have that,' I said, holding out my hand for the ashtray.

In that space of inches, less than inches, Mia let the ashtray go – accidentally or not, I couldn't tell – missing my palm, and it dropped away, as if in escape. We watched it, the two of us, and then I was sweeping up ash, butts and glassy bits of our Las Vegas weekend, as Mia called out her goodbye.

As I had listened for her heels in the hallway that morning in August, now I tried to fill in the sound of her again, in the empty space she'd occupied. I could only hear that word ringing through me: unfulfilled. I was less than this. I was a phony.

With a calculating violence, Stark made cameo appearances in my dreams. Awakening to a cold sweat, heart pounding, I'd move in closer to Carter. More than glad he was there, as he'd once been. When the boys at school slammed me into the cinderblock walls, smeared shit over my locker, drove through my parents' yard, leaving deep rips in the lawn. He'd done his best for me, never yielding, never withdrawing. Would I have taken the same crap for him?

That night, I stumbled out of bed, heart trapped and thudding like a wild animal, and went into the kitchen. On the table, the script, my stained coffee mug (GRADE A HUBBIE), the wilting African violet. A week since I'd sat there, a week since Mia's unexpected visit, two weeks since the reading. Though I'd placed a dozen calls to the producers and directors, I'd received nary a word.

Wanting a cigarette, I searched the freezer, where I usually kept them, without luck. In the dark, I pulled down an ashtray, a simple crystal-cut ashtray, and moved toward the living room, which I'd been avoiding. I stopped in the threshold. A slant of moonlight pierced the window and there were my cigarettes, on the sill where Carter had left them. I seized the pack, aware of that terrible intrusion in the corner, looming and stooped, fingers extended in endless pursuit of the flower. His waxy limbs glimmered in the burst of the match's flame.

'You're really grotesque,' I said.

His contorted face pulsed and I thought his lips twitched into a smile. I moved toward the statue, nothing, no one to keep me from him. To protect him from me. Briefly, I saw the shimmering knife blade cutting, paring, severing. Then, my hands were on him, the smooth wax of his durable skin, my mouth in his ear. *'Hollow motherfuck –'*

'Jed?' Carter, with his floppy, auburn fringe and receding hairline. Shirtless, the paunch of his belly slid indiscreetly over the elastic of his boxers. The orange glow of this world, the city's eternal residue, glazed his face and I saw most definitively the boy he'd been and the man he was.

'Jed, are you all right?' Carter said, raking a hand through his hair.

I walked to the window, cracked it wide, and released the smoke I'd collected in my lungs. The act left me empty, and tired. I lay the cigarette in the ashtray, bluish curlicues rising delicately from the crystal.

'I'm almost forty years old,' I said, rasping.

I didn't feel Carter's hands on my shoulders, nor did I feel the weight of his fingers as they passed over my back. All my efforts concentrated on how I was going to get through it. At last I did feel something, the heat of Carter's body, the familiar terrain of his skin, the gentle tug into the bedroom, where I wrapped myself about him, and shook.

The call came in on Wednesday, at 11:23 a.m. I was sitting at the kitchen table. I spent all of my time in the kitchen now, at the table, smoking one pack of Reds after the other, and staring at the fluttering curtains. The ashtray couldn't conceal the spume of butts and ash, the tips of my fingers and nails dusted grey. I knew what was coming. Who's to say we can't get what we want? After eight years of nothing, finally someone on the

other end, a voice, cool with dollar signs and smouldering with my name.

'Is this Jed Flicker?' he said.

For a second, I thought, Just hang up the phone,
Jedediah, and no one will ever know the difference.
When you've waited as long as I had, there was nothing
else to do but say, 'Yes.'

'Not catching you at a bad time, am I?' he said. 'Don't
want to disturb the creative flow,' chuckling ever so
slightly I knew then who he was. Or rather, who he wasn't.

'Heath Mercer, House of Pain Productions,' he said,
his name already evaporating before it had time to
condense. 'Good work by the way, Jed. Transcendental.'

I struck a key on the typewriter, then another. 'Eight
years,' I said, 'is a long time.'

There was the picture Carter had taken of Mia and
me on the fridge, and behind us, the low, pink-rimmed
sky of Austin. We'd met at a Sigma Nu party (Carter
was a brother), me in my Bermuda shorts and topsiders,
Mia in her green sundress and sandals. There'd been
reggae by 'The Killer Bees', and a game of volleyball in
the front yard and June bugs and kissing in the dark
under the magnolias . . .

'What was that? I missed that last bit.'

'So you called to tell me what exactly?' I said.

'I'd like to take a meeting with you,' he said. 'This
afternoon, if possible.'

'This afternoon,' I said. 'A meeting.' In the
background, the steady ease of traffic, a siren, a horn.
'Where are you calling from?'

'Where am I? I'll tell you where I am,' he said. 'I'm
right here. What do I see? Haze, Jed. Lots of haze and
tall buildings and billboards. The Manhattan skyline,
that's what I see and you know something, it's fantastic.

Nothing like it in the entire world. So how's four o'clock for you?' He spewed out a series of numbers, a prominent address. 'I know you, Jed. You can almost see your name in lights, right?'

I held the phone in my hand, tapped another key, lit another cigarette. The day would go on like this, with the phone ringing and the smoke rising from the ashtray and intermittent thoughts of Mia and of Carter, and I'd lose all trace of the world. My name in lights. 'Jed, you there?'

'Midtown,' I sighed. 'See you then.'

Because I had hours, I decided to walk, for the exercise but also for the sense of leisure it lent. Through the park, I passed all the oily sunbathers and Frisbee throwers, cyclists and skateboarders. The vendors peddling hot-dogs and pretzels, the homeless with their stolen grocery carts full of other people's lives. I hit the East Side, and there was the helical Guggenheim Museum, where Mia and I had attended a Joan Miró retrospective many years ago, our first weekend as an official couple.

When Mia had surprised me with the tickets to New York, I'd said, 'I don't know, Mia. Carter's probably a better choice.' I'd meant it as a joke, since Carter (who wasn't out then) and Mia were both getting a PhD in art history. And I – I was just studying to get by, to bide my time before the bolt hit and I was swept away by inspiration. She'd taken it well. She'd said, smiling, 'He was my first choice, but then I remembered: I'm in love with you, not Carter.' What words for a man like me: a man who could barely keep an intelligent conversation going, a man who felt lost the moment he stepped out his door. I had to wonder, as I'd wondered then, what exactly Mia had seen in me.

Fifth Avenue in summer. The congested, grimy sidewalks of Japanese, German, Spanish, Brazilian tourists, their shoulders colourfully banded by shopping bags. Those see-through bags which held a world of delicacies; cashmere, angora, lace. Christmas presents for friends and family, lovers. The encroaching holidays loomed in shop windows, big calendars full of red Xs marking off the number of days: one hundred and twenty-four.

House of Pain Productions (a subsidiary of Viacom) sat on the forty-fifth floor of a sleek, glass-and-steel tower on Madison Avenue. Heath hadn't lied; the view was spectacular. His office overlooked the park and the buildings lining Central Park West. There was the Dakota, immortalized by John Lennon's assassination and the cult movie classic, *Rosemary's Baby*. How often Mia and I had dreamed of finding ourselves tenants in one of those grand apartments, a place large enough for the family we'd intended. The alpine glow of these buildings, with their white stone gargoyles and glimmering, gilded cupolas, and for a moment, the whole of New York seemed like the invention of Hollywood. Where wives waited on station platforms to be reunited with their husbands and there were no such things as unhappy endings.

'I'm glad you could make it on such short notice,' Heath said, extending his hand to greet me.

He was young, twenty-five years old, if that, his lustreless blue eyes set behind a pair of brushed-steel frames, the lenses minutely scratched. He smelled of the office, of Freon and recycled air and eucalyptus. I saw my life as it might have, should have, been. The hemmed-in cubicle with photographs of Mia tacked up, the coffee mug with pens and paperclips instead of

37

coffee, the workspace cluttered with faxes, memos and meaninglessness. No ashtrays, no smoke, no typewriter. No Manfred Stark. No pilfered story from *The New Yorker*.

Heath offered me a cold soda, and then we drifted down a cool hallway to the conference room. A long, narrow table, a vase of silk flowers, a stack of video cassettes, and a wall of screenplays, alphabetized and catalogued, that reached to the ceiling. Some titles I recognized, most I didn't. 'We're a small company but we do big things,' he said, his arms stretched up and back.

He propped his feet on the table, brown, tasselled loafers spit-shined, the soles scuffed. I thought he might offer me a cigar, as if we were two fresh fathers in a waiting room. Did he have any idea of the caricature he presented to me? This producer, with his slicked-back hair and unwarranted flatteries? This man who saw the future of my script and wanted to pay me for it. Someone else's idea that wasn't even mine to peddle.

For eight years, I'd sat at a table, while Mia and I grew older, further apart. While the world beyond the kitchen revolved and succeeded. Here was someone to make those eight years worthwhile, to give them value and design. To tell me that it was all right I'd pushed aside my marriage, broken from love.

I pictured Stark at the reading, the strange arbitration of our lives. I hadn't seen him in weeks and as I settled further into my seat, becoming more comfortable with my lot, I wondered if I hadn't imagined him all along. Another thought, more likely and more persuasive, telegraphed through me: Mia had lied. That she'd invited him to get back at me.

Even as we discussed plans for *Awful Kisses* and I signed the contract releasing the rights of the script, I felt only regret, the hollow sensation of having missed out on something else, something definite, divine. As if success were a concealed weapon that would go off accidentally in my pocket, leaving another hole.

Over the next few days, I made minor alterations to the script at Heath's request, line edits that he faxed over each morning and expected back the same afternoon. During all of this, I kept expecting Carter to announce his intentions of leaving, but he made none. On occasion, when we happened to climb into bed at the same time, which was rare, I asked him, 'Any news from Hank about the apartment?', though we both knew Hank had already finished the job.

He left messages on the answering machine for Carter, long-winded and apologetic, listing his own deficiencies, pleading with Carter to come home. Then, antagonistic messages about phone calls Carter hadn't returned, cancelled dinners, stand-ups. One about wanting the statue back. And finally, messages hinting at something else, something about Carter and me and his refusal to let it go. Clearly, these last messages I wasn't supposed to intercept. It made me wonder why Carter was still there, when it was more than obvious he had a life with Hank to continue, better or worse.

Although we spoke less, spent fewer hours together, what we said when we eventually did speak, usually in bed, brought us to a different and stranger place. As if the things I was saying to him I should've been saying to Mia. He'd listen, lying on his side, eyes pinned to me in the black. More than once I felt as if he were waiting for me to come to some great decision about him, about us.

Clinging to each other equally in the night, we said nothing in the morning about it. The bed became our momentary silence, a place where the memory of who we used to be, uncomplicated boys with an uncomplicated friendship, thrived. We wrapped ourselves up in Mia's sheets, while the air-conditioner pumped out its arctic air and the sorrows of the day disintegrated. We wouldn't allow them in bed with us, or at least I wouldn't: Carter's ongoing struggle to find the right part, the role that would make him; my insolvency and scattered ennui. I never mentioned that third person in the room, the spectre stationed at the foot of the bed. Nor did I utter Mia's name, Mia who'd taken an apartment in Brooklyn to be closer to school, Mia who'd had her telephone number unlisted.

To find her, I'd have to go through Carter and even at the height of my excitement about the deal I'd made, when I wanted to share my good news, I couldn't bring myself to ask him. After all, hadn't Mia separated and left? Mia who'd called me unfulfilled?

As summer progressed into fall and Carter still had made no murmur of leaving, I wondered if we'd ever truly grown up. If I'd truly ever been married, if he'd ever been with Hank. Years shrank in that tiny apartment, with its buckled linoleum and grey-shaded walls. For what it's worth, I think I must've fallen in some kind of love with the way things were then, those carefree, simplistic mornings when I rose from bed and went into the kitchen, unfettered and wild to begin something new. There was Carter, fixing a breakfast of eggs and toast, making coffee, as though we'd always been like this, a couple. Did loneliness keep us there, some other habit?

But things change with or without permission, and the window that once looked out over the park's sunny dispensation of trees soon looked out over a wasteland of barren limbs and cold, cloudy sky.

One afternoon, after a gruelling day at my typewriter (more last-minute revisions), I took a long run around the reservoir and then went to Lincoln Center to see a movie, *The Glass Key*, starring Veronica Lake and Alan Ladd. (I'm something of a *film noir* buff.) Two hours later, I emerged to drizzle and darkness. The lights of the Metropolitan cast diamond-clustered auras on the wet pavement. Men and women in evening clothes hurried quickly to the doors, where ushers in red suits met them; the ballet had started. As I moved from the plaza, the fountain gushing behind me, the orchestra struck its first chord, and I stopped.

How to describe that moment, when I realized this was my life, that my movie would probably be made, but that I was definitely without Mia. We'd attended the ballet only a few times in our eight years and now I desperately wanted to sit in the dark again with her, to see real people slipping delicately across the stage. I saw Mia, the flimsy projection of our love. How I'd held onto my belief in me only to let go of hers in us.

And I remembered a paper I'd written on the law of parsimony – Occam's Razor – one of the guiding theories of hermeneutics: that to explain otherwise inexplicable phenomena, the simpler of two competing theories must prevail. That people fell in and out of love because that's what happened. That the longer we lived with someone else, the less knowable that someone became. Mia and I had survived in these discrepancies, between the wakeful people we were and the shadowy figures we grew into when asleep, between the kitchen with my daydreams and the bedroom with my nightmares.

By the time I reached the apartment, there was no differentiating among the tears, sweat and water on my face. I let myself inside, my every surface dripping with cold. I passed the sideboard in its usual place against the wall, and on it, the ceramic bowl, the mail neatly stacked.

I called out for Carter, my voice drained and raspy. The wind ravished the blinds in the living room, where he'd forgotten to close the windows. I stood in the threshold, watching the droplets of rain collect in the ashtray, on the sills, spilling over onto the hardwood floor. Not even this could convince me to take a step into that room. I drew a knife from the kitchen and headed for the bedroom.

Shucking off my clothes, I tossed them into the tub. Then, from the closet, emptied of Mia's shoes and dresses, I lugged out a large, heavy cardboard box. In sweeping curls, Mia had written FRAGILE in thick black ink across the top. Dragging the blade through the thick fibrous tape, dusty and coarse, I watched the flaps spring up, as if something inside had been released.

I peered down into a different world – the pages of my half-baked dissertation, course outlines and bulletins, pay stubs from the Department of Philosophy. Everything in a thin veneer of lost time, perfectly preserved with rubber bands and staples, each page bearing the University of Texas's insignia, burnt orange, this perhaps the only thing to have faded.

I was looking for Manfred Stark.

I didn't remember packing any of it, had thought I'd left it all behind. The afternoon Mia and I had abandoned our small cottage on 29th Street and Rio Grande, piling her suitcases and my duffel bags into the trunk, beginning a drive of fifteen hundred odd miles to New York that would take us three days. But there it was, my life in scraps and letters and memos, encapsulated and pristine, a historian's approximate reconstruction of a life: Jed Flicker's promising early years.

I felt a brimming sadness as I pulled the contents out of the box. Mementos, souvenirs of the man I'd been, a photograph I'd caught of Mia unawares at Deep Eddy pool, the menu of our favourite restaurant, Red River Café (the best green enchiladas in all of Austin). And Carter, his letter informing me that he'd be moving to New York to pursue acting, our high school graduation programme with our names stuck one on top of the other: Flicker, Gilford.

Sifting through it all, I came upon an old short story of mine: about a fifteen-year-old boy who accidentally hits a ten-point buck in his father's Mercedes, then must decide how to put the buck out of its misery. Which he eventually does by running over it, puncturing one of the tyres on an antler. A heavy-handed, terrible story. My father hadn't ever lent me his car, nor had I ever hit a buck. What did I know about it, much less about killing? I suppose I was trying to say something about the unexpected, that lonely dirt road in the middle of the night.

I found my eight-year-old copy of *The New Yorker*, the one with 'The Cheerleader's Kiss'. The cover came off in my hands, the pages brittle as my imagination. Though I'd looked, he'd never had another one printed in the magazine. Though I'd searched the shelves of many bookstores in the city, I never found him. It didn't seem possible this was his only story, the only one that lived.

Manfred Stark was out there somewhere, in that vast cold rainfall, seething and vengeful. Why else show up to a closed reading unexpectedly? Hadn't I, in some way, been inviting this for years?

The door to the apartment swung open, announcing Carter. Quickly, I dumped all the papers, memorabilia, and magazines back into the box. I was sliding the box into the closet when Mia appeared in the doorway, wet as a bedraggled cat.

Her hair hung in her face, the curls loosened by the weight of the water. Drops rolled and plunged off her, puddling at her feet. We stood there, saying nothing, me with that ghastly linchpin in hand, she with her tote.

At last, Mia said, glancing at the box, 'Carter was mugged,' but something in her face told me this wasn't the end. 'He was stabbed, Jed.'

I slunk down onto the bed. 'What? What are you saying?' I said. 'Carter's at work, Mia, where he always is.'

'I was there, at the bar, having a drink, and then we were leaving and this man . . .' Her voice trailed off, a flicker of sorrow. 'This man . . .'

'Where is he?' I said, springing to the closet for my overcoat. 'What hospital, Mia?' She shook her head. 'Where, Mia?'

The night burst with delirious white streaks and the rain blowing in through the open window, dowsing the pickled-pine table, my typewriter, mug, script, cigarettes, the habits that made me who I was. I felt Mia at my back, the tendrils of her fingers, hot rapid breath against my neck.

'He's at Mount Sinai,' she said softly. 'He's going to be all right.'

'The man who did it,' I said. 'Was he the same guy at the reading? Did you see his face?'

'He was just a man, Jed,' Mia said, looking at me

strangely, as if she'd never seen me before. 'Nothing special about him at all.'

I wanted to go to Carter immediately but Mia persuaded me otherwise. 'We'll go together, tomorrow,' she said.

She stayed the night and we slept as if she'd never left. In the morning, the sun spilled through the thin tissue of clouds, crossing into the room, this room we'd shared for eight years. For an instant, we were exactly as we'd always been, Mia and I, even better. I'd rise as I usually did, at six, pad into the kitchen, and fix a pot of coffee. That first morning cigarette, that first key struck. Mia hadn't decided to leave me yet, Carter hadn't moved in and I hadn't forsaken my dissertation to become the selfish husband and friend I would turn out to be. This was a moment, and it evaporated the second I opened my eyes.

I went into the kitchen, the air frigid, the floor spotted with ice. My breath left my body, tiny cottony bursts. A multitude of icicles hung off the table, thin as straws. When the sun hit the table's top, everything, typewriter, pack of cigarettes, script, sparkled with ice.

I tried to force the window shut but it wouldn't close. I got a knife from the drawer and as I chipped away at the ice, thin shavings immediately turning to water, I thought of Carter and understood then that there were invisible designs laid out for all of us, as intricate as snowflakes, simple as raindrops. Each design inimitable, irrefutable. Could I have done anything differently? If I had, would I have been the same man I was that second?

Ten minutes later, I shut the window, listening to Mia stir in the other room. She called out my name and I saw us, years from then, in a new apartment, with children. I stood in the threshold of the living room, the sun breaking through the grimy windows. In the corner, where the statue had been, two waxy footprints on the hardwood floor. I didn't have any inkling where it had gone, only that it was. Maybe Hank had come by to reclaim it, maybe Carter had dismantled it and one day, I'd find hidden traces – filaments, cathodes, pinwheel – throughout the apartment. Or maybe, like some creations, it had simply gotten up and left.

I closed the windows, the ice having already softened in the sun. The crystal-cut ashtray, brimming with water and soggy butts, sat in the same place on the sill. I thought of Manfred Stark, what I'd taken from him, what he'd taken from me. I thought of his story, 'The Cheerleader's Kiss'. How awful Gus Snyder had found the girl's kisses, her breath like wet leaves, and how wrong his assumptions had been about her – that even at her young age, she'd expressed such monstrous ambition. I saw myself then, in morning's full bright-ness, and I wasn't Gus, as I'd always imagined, but that cheerleader, seducing and promising and caroming my way through the world. How could I not but understand my own selfish drives, capitalizing on another man's idea, inviting Carter into my bed, allowing Mia to disappear so easily?

I moved to the doorway and there she was, in the threshold of the bedroom, flattened hair, lopsided breasts, the same rosy birthmark on her right shoulder. She said my name again, her lips seemingly unmoving and shaded dark in the sun. We stood there, blinking and smiling at each other, in that apartment with so much and so little of us – the sideboard, our keys and stacks of mail, the telephone bill in her name, the electric bill in mine, the simplest things, our habits and our love.

# a perfect day for swimming

In December, I went to visit my father in Austin because Alex had just left me, I'd quit my assistant editing job at *Glamour*, and I wanted to be someplace that wasn't New York in winter. I went because my mother wasn't an option. She and her creepy husband, Ted, were travelling to Jekyll Island off the coast of Georgia, where Ted's family had a house. I went because I had no other place to go.

'Spend Christmas with us, Kate,' my father had said and I'd thought, Why not? Sun, margaritas, *and* a heart-shaped swimming pool.

He sprung for my ticket, and arranged for a car to pick me up at the airport. He sounded strange on the phone, as if he hadn't slept in days. Because my father's an attorney, hard-working and harder-drinking, I didn't think anything of it. I simply thought he was immersed in a case.

I arrived at the house, knocked on the door, rang the bell. Nothing, no one. I sweated like a tropical forest in my black cable-knit, turtleneck sweater, black wool pants, black boots. A fixed, hot sun, and the temperature in the low eighties. Winter days in Austin.

I called out, 'Dad? Howard?' I called out, 'Matthew? Jason?' (Howard's kids from his first marriage.) No one came to the door or the windows or zoomed around from behind the house. 'Jesus,' I mumbled.

Suitcase in hand, I headed around to the back yard and tried the deck door, which was locked. Inside, the kitchen glimmered, white and spotless. A bottle of Chivas Regal, a red velvet bow tied at its throat, sat on the tiled counter. A defrosting turkey, probably thirty pounds, perched on the table, drops of oily water catching the falling slants of sunlight. 'Howard? Dad?' I said again, tapping the glass. Two o'clock in the afternoon, I thought. Where the hell is everybody?

I called the house on my cellphone and Howard's deep voice emanated from the answering machine. 'Howdy-ho,' he said cheerily. 'We can't come to the phone . . .'

'No doubt,' I said, and sank down into one of the deckchairs, removing my sweater and unzipping my boots.

It had been snowing in Brooklyn, drifting by our fourth-storey windows, when Alex had announced he was moving out. I'd thrown the bottle of wine I'd been drinking at him and said, 'Something I said?' I knew it was more than that; I was just being a bitch. We'd been living together for three years and I expected a little more from him, like not breaking up with me when we're scheduled to spend the holidays in Cancun.

Opening my suitcase, I found my hot-pink, string bikini and stripped. I gathered up my Walkman and headed to the pool. The sun made me feel babyish and stiff, as if I'd recently emerged from a coma. I laid out on one of the loungers for about half an hour. The sun

roasted the air, flies buzzed, my head spun. I saw Alex
carrying boxes out, shaking his head as I'd sat on the
couch, smoking and drinking. I knew why he was going.
At one point, he'd sat down beside me and said, 'You
could've done anything else, Kate, anything at all. But
you didn't.' He was talking about his maps, which I'd
ripped to shreds the night before. Alex collected maps:
old maps, rare and expensive maps. Maps of Africa and
Asia and Russia. Gorgeous maps with blues and greens
and browns. Hundreds of maps.

Sufficiently fried, I went to the lip of the pool and
dabbed my foot in the tepid water. I plucked off my sun-
glasses, knelt down, and let out a little gasp, which in
turn became a series of hard giggles. Because there, lying
on the bottom, was Santa Claus.

A shiny red Explorer pulled into the driveway, windows
down. Singing cut through the patchy suburban quiet: *If
you stay, it'll get better/Wherever you go it's bound to
rain.* Matthew and Jason bolted out of the car, hooting,
and fell onto the grass, clutching their necks. 'Country
music sucks,' they said in unison.

Howard called, 'Boys, straws suck, country music
does not. Now, take the bags inside, please.' The sun
had fallen behind the trees, shading the pool. As I
climbed off the raft, forgetting about Santa, my foot
hit a corner of the plastic and I winced, though I felt
nothing acutely. I wrapped myself in a towel and headed
up to the house. The boys sang, 'Kate's here, Kate's
here,' then darted off. Howard met me on the wooden
deck, sweating lightly.

'Kate,' he said, wrapping me in a bear-hug, 'so good
to see you. Have you been here long?'

'Long enough to take a dip in your heart,' I said,

shaking my hair loose of the remaining water. 'And long enough to find Santa. Howard, what's going on?'

His face became a bundle of untidy energy, which on some men might have been interpreted as excitement; on Howard, it seemed nervous. We went into the cool kitchen. His meaty hands reached into the brown-paper bags, extracting steaks, bacon, rice cakes. Sweat clung lightly to the pock-marked skin around his ears. Beneath his T-shirt, his cannonball-like shoulders and barrel-chest professed hours spent in the gym. He wore a green fatigue T-shirt with the word SEAL, in bold black piping. The shirt, like Howard, had seen a lot. He might've been handsome if he weren't my father's lover.

'So that's where your father dumped Santa,' Howard said sadly. 'Kate, Doug and I had a falling out. He moved into the Four Seasons in town. He was supposed to have telephoned you.'

'No telephone,' I said.

Howard walked over to the turkey, poked it with a finger. 'God, I knew I should've bought fresh this year,' he said, noticing something on the floor. He turned around and said, 'Kate, are you bleeding?'

I looked down at a couple of blotchy red footprints. I lifted up my right foot and there, on the soft fleshy arch, a tiny crooked gash. I laughed a meandering laugh; honestly, I felt nothing.

'Boys,' Howard called, 'take Kate upstairs and show her where the antibacterial soap is.' He squeezed one of my shoulders. 'You'll be all right, kiddo. Not life-threatening.'

The boys were playing *Star Wars* on the stairs. Matthew was Yoda; Jason, Luke Skywalker. Matthew, the younger, said, 'You're a coward, Skywalker.'

Jason replied, 'Up yours, Yoda.'

In the living room, on the mantel, there was a picture of me at Lost Maples National Park, in a pair of wet shorts, with long hair. I'd taken the photo beside it, of Howard and my father kissing, a few years back. Beneath the photographs, four oversized stockings tacked up. An unadorned giant Christmas tree stood in the corner by the door. The whole room smelled of pine and popcorn. Other than the picture, no further signs of my father anywhere.

Matthew said, 'I broke my foot once.' He smiled and touched my big toe. Then he leaned down and planted a tiny kiss there. Although the accident had occurred a few months ago, Matthew measured its passing in adventure – trips to the zoo, the circus, the Ice Capades. The minutiae of his life fascinated me, mainly because it all unfolded in the same sweet earnest way. There was no trying, only the glory of play. To be six years old again, I thought.

'I remember,' I said. 'But that was an accident and you were such a big boy.'

Jason grimaced. He'd had longer to process the nasty world of adults and knew that Matthew's 'accident' might not have been an accident at all. The jury was still out on exactly what had happened; only Matthew knew for sure. I could sense Jason's burgeoning rage as he moped around the room, picking up a neon-green toy water gun cracked in two.

'I broke this,' he said grinning. 'Doug gave it to me on my birthday but I can't use it anymore. I asked Santa Claus for a new one but he's dead.'

Matthew said, huffily, 'Nuh-uh, Jathon. Santa's not dead. He'th just – not there.'

I couldn't help smiling at Matthew; when I was his

age, I'd had the same trouble controlling my esses. Especially when I was frustrated.

Jason shrugged, dropped the gun on the carpet amid a pile of clothes and ratty *X-Men* comic books. His restlessness was abstracted. I wanted to grab him by the shoulders and hold him still. I said, 'Jason, why don't you come over here and play with us?'

His brown eyes turned toward the window with light expectation, as a car turned into the driveway. When the car pulled out again a moment later, the expectation fizzled into anger. He fidgeted at the window, tapping it absently with his fingers, a drummer banging out a song.

'Hey, guys. I have a great idea. Why don't you surprise your dad and clean up your rooms?' I said, trying not to sound like a game-show hostess, the mother they didn't have and probably needed. My voice felt stagy, full of booby prizes and trapdoors. Just play the game, boys, and see how much you can win.

'Only if I can have some Nerds,' Matthew said.

'I'll see what I can do,' I said, rising.

Jason tugged at my back and indicated for me to kneel down. Then, he whispered, 'When Matthew broke his foot, Doug gave him these little blue pills. Want me to get some for you?'

I looked over at the plaster cast of Matthew's tiny foot on the shelf, displayed between his World Series baseball signed by Bernie Williams and his Little League trophy, third place.

'No thanks,' I said. 'I'm perfectly fine.'

Jason grimaced again. Of course you're not fine, his face said. I turned my back on him. When the pain finally did come, there would be something comforting in it, something useful and familiar.

*

Downstairs, Howard spoke quietly on the phone. He held up a hand, motioning to the refrigerator, nearly hidden behind a collage of decorations and drawings made by the boys. Happy-face magnets of shellacked bread dough, stick figures in different coloured pencil, with glitter for lips and sequins for eyes. Warped and blotchy watercolours of dead deer and rifles. Two lists, both to Santa, each an entire page long. On my own fridge at home, there was simply an ancient black-and-white wedding photograph of my mother and father.

The coffee still too hot, I added some ice, a lot of sugar and cream. I went outside to the deck. I heard, 'No, Doug, we've talked about this already. You can stay to trim the tree and *then you go*.'

Howard came out, face tight, hands shaking as he stirred his coffee. 'How's your foot?' he said.

I nodded that it was all right as he reached over to examine it. 'Your father's on his way.' He massaged my foot absently. I sat there, letting him, because really, why not? It felt great. Howard gave great massages, better than anyone. Once, a couple years ago, I told Alex this and he said, 'Of course. Being a fag makes him sensitive that way.' I didn't know. Things like that were hard to say. Howard drank beer, played softball, worked out in the yard. He also gave incredible foot rubs. It seemed to me that my father had it pretty good.

'How are the boys holding up?' I said.

'Oh, well, they're confused,' Howard said. 'Like me. Like the entire world when something like this happens. Don't let anyone tell you that men are from Mars and women are from Venus, Kate. Everyone's from Pluto.'

Tentatively, I said, 'What about Jason?'

'What do you mean?' Howard said. 'Did he – oh, God, he didn't do anything to Matthew again, did he?

I've told him a thousand times not to be a bully. I'm so afraid he's going to turn into –' There was real surprise in his voice and behind that, something pinched and strained.

'No, no, nothing like that. He's just, well, he seems a little angry to me,' I said.

'He's angry, Kate. We're all angry. The only one of us who isn't angry is Matthew and he's not old enough yet to realize it. When your father –'

'Howard, that was an accident,' I said. 'Wasn't it?'

'You mean like Santa in the swimming pool,' he said, shaking his head in earnest. 'If you only knew, Kate.'

I knew a little. I knew my father came home drunk and stayed drunk the entire evening. I knew that he let his law practice run itself, which meant he wasn't paying his bills or employees. I knew he'd been calling me, his only daughter, at all hours of the night, crying.

Unable to sit still, Howard rose and wandered over to a potted geranium. He buried a finger in it. 'I really have to water this more or it's a goner.'

I sat in silence, sipping my coffee. 'What did he do this time?' I said.

'Nothing,' Howard said. 'Everything. You know Doug's drill, Kate. Two months of flowers and kindness and then *wham!* we're back in the trenches with him.'

The door flew open and Jason and Matthew tore out of the house. Their light-sabres, one orange, one green, iridescent in the crepuscular dark. 'Boys, for heaven's sake,' Howard said.

'I cleaned my room,' Matthew said. 'Can I have my Nerds now?'

Howard frowned. 'Bribery went out with Barney the Dinosaur,' he said to me. I smiled tensely. 'Sugar is our new war,' he added as my father pulled his truck into the driveway.

The boys lost their sabres and raced over to it. A couple of minutes later, they flanked my father, swinging his arms back and forth. Without his beard, his face looked sunken and lost.

'Doug's here,' Matthew said.

Jason let go my father's hand and stood away from them, holding up his little hands, as if trying to keep something from falling on top of him. He made a series of squeaks.

'Jason, stop that please,' Howard said.

'I'm trying to locate Santa,' he said. 'I think I picked up his signal. It's very weak . . .'

'I don't care if you're speaking to Ghengis Khan, cease and desist right this minute,' Howard said, smiling. Look at my boy, his face said. Tell me he's not going to be all right.

'Hello, Doug,' Howard said, neither warm nor pleasant.

'Howard,' my father said, peering past him into the house.

'I'll get started on dinner,' Howard said, smoothing out his I GET A KICK OUT OF YOU apron. 'Boys, set the table for dinner please.'

'No need,' my father said. 'Rudy's BBQ to the rescue.'

'Then I guess I'll go and take a shower,' Howard said and went inside.

I said, turning to my father, 'How are you holding up?'

'About as good as I can be,' he said, 'considering this is the third day in a row I've thought about hanging myself with my own entrails.'

'That isn't funny,' I said. And then, 'Why didn't you call me?'

'I thought I could fix it before you got here,' he said. 'And you're right. That's not funny.' He paused. 'Not nearly as funny as your fifty-two-year-old father staring at himself in the mirror on Christmas Eve and wondering how the hell he's made such a mess of his life.'

His speech was warm and liquid and I wondered if he'd been drinking. I leaned into him, only to catch the whiff of garlic, and behind that, peppermint.

'Well, even if Howard isn't glad you're here, I am,' I said, the pain in my foot livid. I went to the door.

'Kate, what's with the limp?' he said.

'I stepped on Santa Claus in the pool,' I said.

My father wrinkled up his face. 'Yes, that's one of the casualties,' he said. 'Are you all right?' I nodded. 'It's good to see you, daughter. I'm looking forward to our little outing on Sunday.'

'Me, too,' I said. We'd planned a camping trip to Lost Maples, a place I hadn't been since girlhood.

'Well, then, I'll get the spare ribs – hickory-smoked, your favourite – out of the car,' he said.

I gave him a great big smile, teeth and all. I didn't feel like reminding him I hadn't touched red meat in years.

During dinner, the phone rang twice. My father excused himself and I heard him above us, creaking across the hardwood floors. I was on my third gin and tonic when he reappeared and said, 'Howard, Jerome beeped in. He said something about bridge next week. I told him you'd call him back.'

Howard said, 'Bridge. Don't make me laugh.'

My father rubbed his hands together as if he were

about to perform a magic trick. And now here's Douglas Burnett, HOUDINI'S HOMOSEXUAL COUSIN. He said, 'Which of my big boys wants to help me trim the tree?'

'Me, Doug, me. I do, Doug. Let me. I'm older,' Jason said.

'But I'm Yoda,' Matthew said, face stormy. 'That maketh me older by a thousand yearth!'

'Say years,' Jason said, taking the initiative, goading. Something Jason had obviously heard before. 'Say it, Matthew. Years, not yearth.'

Matthew shook his head, lowered his eyes. 'No.'

'Please, boys, enough. Go help Doug,' Howard said, massaging his temples.

I looked at him, this worn-out man, who for ages had endured the bloody, damaged Burnett heart next to him. Almost as a reflex, my father placed a hand on Howard's shoulder. The boys' faces, like my own, waffled between consternation and wonder. My father leaned down and planted a kiss on the bald crown of Howard's head.

'Doug,' Howard said, 'come on.'

'Angel angel angel,' the boys sang, racing around the table.

I sat silent, taking in this unsettling tableau.

'Stay close to your father,' Howard said. 'And Doug, the light's out in the garage so take this.' He handed my father a flashlight. As he held it out and my father took it, Howard's eyes gently drifted over his face, his own face changing incrementally, from disappointment to acknowledgement to something else entirely. It said, *I see you're trying but it's not enough*.

With my father and the boys outside, Howard said, 'Your father looks . . .'

Like a train wreck, I thought. 'He still loves you, Howard,' I said.

'Oh, I know that,' he said. 'But that isn't the point. Love can't keep this marriage from imploding.'

'What about counselling?' I said.

'Tried it,' he sighed. 'But after Doug punched Father Louden and broke his glasses, I asked myself why in the heck I was going through this with him. Your father's not an easy man to get along with.'

'No offence but that doesn't sound like him,' I said, running a finger around the lip of the glass. 'He was never violent with me or –'

'Well, like it or not,' Howard said, face flushed in the light, 'that's what happened.'

Somewhere, beyond the perimeter of the house, the boys scattered as my father called them back. I finished my drink, poured another, and then went down to the steamy, heated pool.


Howard and my father gathered around the tree, while Matthew sat on the floor working on a string of cranberries. His little fingers, stained red, waved up at me. Jason, his breathing insistent through a Darth Vader mask, marched from fire to tree, tree to kitchen, kitchen to fire again.

'Kate, you're just in time for the angel,' my father said. 'Howard, the angel, please.'

Howard looked around him. 'I thought you brought it in,' he said.

'I must've left her in the car,' my father said. 'Kate, how about –'

'No, no, no,' Howard said. 'You stay here. I need to grab some cranberry sauce out of the freezer in the garage.' My father tossed Howard the keys. 'Jason, if

I've told you once, I've told you a thousand times, get your butt away from the fire.'

Mesmerized, his entire body finally at rest, Jason watched the logs break apart. The flue sucked up the glowing embers in a dazzling swirl. 'You know, this is the first time since I've been here that you've actually stopped moving,' I said, tousling his hair.

'He's a mover and a shaker,' my father said. 'No harm in that.'

I said, 'What happened to the star we used to have?'

'Up in flames,' my father said. 'Last year.'

'I made that star,' I said.

'Wait until you see the angel,' my father said. 'Howard's grandmother's. I had it cleaned.'

'Thugar, thugar, thugar,' Matthew said and shook the bag of Nerds I'd found for him hidden in the pantry.

'Say sugar,' my father said. 'S-u-g-a-r.'

'That'th what I thaid,' he said. 'Eth-u-g-a-r.'

'Where in the heck one of these boys picked up a lisp, I'll never know,' my father said.

'Maybe you'd like to blame that on me, too,' Howard said, standing in the door, angel in one hand, an empty bottle of whiskey in the other. His face was missing its usual out-in-the-yard tan. 'Doug,' he said, 'I'd like you to go now.'

The air in the room tautened and I shifted uncomfortably. Matthew stopped threading the cranberries and threw them at Jason, who launched them into the fire. Too hot, they exploded, like bullets.

'Howard, what are you babbling about?' my father said.

Howard set the angel down on the coffee table. 'I found this,' he said, 'on the floor in the back of your truck.'

My father's face registered a frown. 'That's an old bottle, Howard,' he said. 'Now, will someone please hand me the angel?'

'No, Doug,' Howard said. 'You have to go.'

Jason picked up the angel and turned it over, while Howard and my father's bickering grew operatic. Their voices rose, heavy, muscular, each word lifting the hairs on my neck. Matthew scooted up against the couch and covered his ears. I knelt down beside him and stroked the smooth skin of his cheek. The melodrama unfolded like a bad TV movie. Howard stormed out of the room and went into the kitchen. I heard him speaking on the phone, though I had no idea with whom.

My father, still on the ladder, rested his head against a rung, staring off at the pool, unaware of Jason below him. Standing at the ladder's foot, Jason reached up to hand my father the angel, opened his hands, and let it go. I tried to yell, 'Dad,' but my voice wouldn't leave my body. My father reached for the angel, which slipped out of his fingers, somersaulted to the floor and shattered. My head filled with the staged gasps of a live TV audience.

Howard rushed back in and said, 'Ooh, my angel,' and turned to Jason, who was halfway up the stairs.

My father scrambled down the ladder, stepping over the broken, jagged pieces, fury in his eyes.

'She's ruined,' Howard said.

'Get back here,' my father said, and lunged for Jason. He snagged the boy in his paws.

Matthew burrowed his brown head into my shoulder and shuddered, his little body going rigid. Staring at my father, whose hands were on Jason's shoulders, both faces slack and blank, Howard said, 'Get. Your. Hands. Off. My. Child.' His voice, doused in gasoline, needed just another word from my father to help it combust.

My father let go Jason, who bolted up the stairs. 'This is my house,' my father roared. 'My house, Howard. My landscape, my pool, my furniture.'

Without saying a word, I led Matthew out of the room and then went to check on Jason. In the dark, he sat on his bed, clutching a Luke Skywalker doll in one hand, a Princess Leia doll in the other.

'You really screwed up this time,' Leia said. 'It wasn't me,' Luke said. 'It was the dark side.'

'Jason,' I said, entering his room.

'Go away,' he said. 'I'm busy.'

'Jason, it wasn't your fault,' I said. Howard and my father's voices sifted up to us. Something smashed, something else was knocked over, a door slammed. 'This has nothing to do with you.'

'But I did it on purpose,' he said.

Throwing the dolls against the wall, his little body shook and then he was crying. I sat down next to him and wrapped him in my arms. Matthew came in and then the three of us huddled together on the bed in the dark until my father's truck screeched out of the driveway.

Sometime during the night, Howard had laid out all the boys' presents. A plate of chocolate chip cookies, half-eaten, sat on the sideboard beside a half-drunk glass of milk. The tree lifeless, unlit lights and silver balls, strings of cranberries, popcorn, tinsel. I plugged the cord in. I drank the rest of the milk.

Standing at the window, I looked toward the pool, wisps of steam curling into the chilly night air. There was my father swimming laps, the bottle of Chivas resting on the pool's lip, glinting in the moonlight. The

61

house lay silent, holding its breath as I made my way to him. I waited while he swam up and down the length of the heart. When he saw me, he said, 'This is my house, daughter. My pool, my fucking business.'

'Dad, Howard keeps threatening to get a restraining order.'

He laughed and climbed out, shivering. He dried off his naked body, surprisingly well maintained. 'Let Howard try,' he said, cinching the towel about his waist and staring up at the house. 'I love that guy, you know. And those kids.'

'I know,' I said. 'They love you, too.'

'They shouldn't,' he said, and reached for the Chivas. 'Share a drink with your old man?'

He took a swig and passed me the bottle. I took one, too, a healthy gulp. The flavour of it, strong and medicinal, exploded in my mouth. 'Only the best,' he said, 'for my Kate.'

I smiled. How could I possibly be angry at my poor wreck of a father? There he was, charming and defective, life's incongruities playing their sad melodies in his head. I knew this, because life's incongruities were playing in mine as well.

'It's freezing out here,' I said, rising.

Inside, we sat at the kitchen table, speaking in whispers. My father played with the pieces of the angel spread out before us. 'What a Christmas,' he said, lifting up one of the blue porcelain wings. 'What a disaster.'

It was then that I thought of Alex and the butterfly, which I'd stayed up all night gluing together out of the pieces of his maps. He'd left that behind as well.

'Nothing's unfixable,' I said.

He said, 'Ah, but is it worth the fixing? Now that I think is the real question.' He gulped from the bottle, his big horsey brown eyes staring past me to the refrigerator. I knew he was weighing the possibilities, the maybes, the if-thens. His face grew stern, a complexity of motion in his head. Then he rose and went rifling through the kitchen drawers. 'That Krazy glue's in here somewhere,' he said.

'No, dad,' I said. 'I was thinking more of Target, you know.'

'Target,' he said, forgoing the search. 'Kate, you're a genius.'

I am my father's daughter, I thought. While he dressed, I called my voice mail: a message from my mother and Ted wishing me a merry Christmas. Nothing from Alex. My father returned and said, 'Okay, so how're we going to get there?'

'Let's take your truck,' I said. 'I'll drive.'

He shook his head. 'Can't,' he said. His face went flaccid and he brought the bottle to his lips. 'It's resting out on Highway 2222. Nothing major, but it won't run. No gas.'

'How did you get here, then?' I said in disbelief.

'Walked,' he said.


At two o'clock in the morning, we stepped into Target. Bright and antiseptic but soothing, with its familiar buzz of fluorescent lights, its holiday Muzak. Everything glowed that underwater blue, as silent sirens announced sudden holiday specials. The beauty and calm of this place were matched only by my own, helped along by the Chivas, which my father had managed to smuggle in. He was an extraordinary specimen.

Needing to use the bathroom, I said, 'Don't go wandering off, dad.'

He smiled, raised three fingers, and said, 'Lawyer's honour.'

By the time I got out, he was gone of course. I headed directly to the Christmas tree ornament aisle. No luck there. I scanned the rows of ornaments, gold stars with fake peridots and Plexiglas stars with green sand and *Joyeux Noël* in red. I took one of the gold stars and left the aisle. I called out his name, softly at first, then louder. The instrumental chorus to 'O Come, All Ye Faithful' jammed my head as I wandered from aisle to aisle, up one and down another. He was nowhere.

Twenty minutes later, after having him paged without result, I found him behind the wheel of the Explorer. Another gold star sat on the seat beside him, glittering in the sodium lamp's orange halo. He said, 'Toss me the keys, Kate,' and I fought the urge to remind him that he'd already lost one car that night.

'Where'd you disappear to?' I said, placing the gold stars on the back seat.

'I thought you said to meet you here,' he said.

'Dad,' I said and climbed in. Perhaps out of exhaustion, perhaps out of some misguided notion I had of fathers and daughters, that safety was inherent in the deal, I handed the keys to him and said, 'Nothing fancy, just drive.'

He grinned and crossed his fingers over his chest. I should've flexed what little authority I had, since I was the one who'd left Howard the note telling him that I'd borrowed his car. Yet the idea of arguing with my father, the defence attorney, at this late hour, seemed moot.

'How about we stop off for a teensy-weensy little drink to toast my daughter's brilliance?' he said, manoeuvring Howard's car down South Congress, the capital building at our backs. My father, the lush, I thought. He took a right onto Fourth Street and headed over to Colorado. We passed a bar, the Boathouse, and he turned into the alley. 'No sense paying to park,' he added.

Once inside, it became clear my father was a regular. The men nodded and grinned at him as we passed. Some leaned on the mirrored walls, others danced on the tiny, elevated dance floor. Catching me, their faces went slack, their eyes glazing over, as if they'd never seen a woman before. Immediately, I resented my father's choice in venues, almost as much as I resented myself for having been coerced. I said, 'One drink, and then we're out of here. Right?'

'Anything, daffodil,' he said, cosying up to the bar.

The bartender, a big-boned man in overalls, smiled when he saw my father and said, 'I swear on the ghost of Norma Jean Baker, counsellor, I'm innocent.' He held up his hands in mock surrender.

'Howdy, Sid,' my father said. 'Sid, my lovely daughter, Kate.'

'Delighted,' Sid said and poured out three shots of peppermint schnapps, two of which he slid to us. 'Pleased to make your acquaintance.'

We lifted our glasses, clinked in succession, and downed the schnapps, which tasted corrosive, like fermented mouthwash. I asked for a glass of water and a beer while my father ordered a scotch, neat, and said, 'I'll be right back.'

He wobbled toward the back of the bar and disappeared through a door marked COXSWAINS. Then, it was simply me and my beer and the thrashing men who stared at themselves in the mirrors. At one point, Sid said, 'Doug tells me you're from Brooklyn?'

I shook my head, having only caught the last part – from Brooklyn. I said, 'Me and the boyfriend broke up,' as if this might explain the reason I was standing in a gay bar on Christmas morning.

'Terrible news,' Sid said. 'He cheat on you or something?'

'Alex was faithful,' I said, the words working their way out of me like splinters.

'Because you know, that's what men do: they cheat,' Sid said. 'I come from a long line of cheaters myself. It's in my blood, I suppose. Hard to change it once it's there, you know what I'm saying.'

I nodded. Yes, I knew. As I drank my beer and searched the faces of these good-looking, well-dressed men, I saw something new, some inexplicable sadness. As if for a moment, drunk and twirling, the future had opened up to them, full of empty rooms and emptier beds. I'd caught this same expression on my face sometimes, in the mirror at work, a darkened window, and it frightened me. It was my father's face.

Minutes later, my father returned with a boy who couldn't have been more than twenty years old. 'Daffodil, I'd like you to meet . . .' He leaned in and whispered something into the boy's ear.

'Chad,' the boy said, extending his hand. 'I'm on the university's swim team.'

We all laughed nervously at his *non sequitur*. His hand, festooned with silver rings, curled dense in my own. The air around him smelled of chlorine and potato chips. My father finished his drink and ordered another for himself and one for Chad, who'd taken up a position between us. He was a tall, gaunt boy, with blond spiky hair, the hoops in his ears glinting in the dim light cast by the eruption of lighters. I liked him, though I couldn't say why.

My father stared at him, enraptured, and compassion

rolled over inside of me. I felt it then, what it must've been like to be my father, going from one failed relationship to the next, his last one moribund, if not already dead. I knew then there were worse things than infidelity, worse even than skipping out on love: the surrender of what you had for the promise of what you didn't. A tighter fit, a more winning smile. Someone else, someone better. I thought of Alex, the challenge and bliss of being with someone who'd put up with me for three years, his persistence as foreign as the names of the cities covering his maps.

At some point, Chad and my father drifted away, let loose upon a whorl of passion. I stood there, sipping my beer, while my father danced with this boy less than half his age. Something appalling and beautiful in it, the way their bodies met in that space. My father's big and burly, the boy's unrestricted and severe. I thought of Lost Maples, the giant trees with their golden leaves. There'd be no camping trip, no hiking, no swimming. There'd only be what there'd always been: my father and his heart.

Chad appeared beside me and said, 'Come dance with us,' and I shook my head no.

'I hurt my foot,' I said, though this wasn't it at all.

'Your dad's really fun,' he said. His wide, freckled face held the most pleasant and knowing of grins. 'We're going to take off pretty soon, I guess. Nice to meet you.' And then he drifted off again.

I shifted all my weight to my foot, to feel the pain, resplendent and alive, to feel anything but the abstraction of a much fiercer longing. As a familiar song came on and the dance floor filled up, I ordered another beer, while my father and this lovely boy, this swimmer, spun each other around, dizzying and graceful. They made it look so easy, this coming together. Maybe that's all there is, I thought, moving from the bar toward the perimeter of the floor, where I joined the crush of handsome men who glanced right through me.

# lana turner slept here

Yawning, I turn my face away from the spotty window
of our bedroom, and touch Achilles's cleaved chin.
Beyond our small, untidy apartment, here in this
run-down neighbourhood in Los Angeles, the sky settles
into a gentle rolling blue. The weather report siphons
out of the clock radio – another day of sunshine – and I
groan. Next to me, Achilles scratches his chin in his
sleep. Usually, I find this adorable, but this morning, I'm
too nervous to find anything adorable. Not the mole on
his right cheek; not his thick, blue-black eyelashes; not
the scar under his left eye. I'm a wreck. This is the day, I
think, rolling out of bed and into my slippers. This is the
day I'm going to spot my brother, Noam.

I glide into the kitchen, set up the kettle, light the
stove. I scoop out five large tablespoons of El Pico
espresso, arrange two mugs on the table, one with four
sugars and cream; the other, for me, with a dash of
cinnamon, the same colour as Achilles's silk boxers.

The truth is this: I still have a problem thinking of
myself as the kind of woman who'd fall for a guy who
wears silk anything but here I am, in Achilles's kitchen.

Here I am, in a city I don't care for, getting ready for a job I don't care for either.

The kettle lets out a wimpy whistle. I look up and, on schedule, Achilles and his early morning erection stand in the doorway. He rakes a hand through his jungle of black curly hair and I wince. No man should ever have more hair than the woman he's sleeping with; Achilles does. My hair's falling out by the handful. Soon, I'll cave in and start that Propecia treatment Fionna keeps hocking me about. It's in my contract: if I lose any more hair, it's time for the wig. I hate the thought of putting someone else's hair on my head. So it's the Propecia or nothing.

We make love quickly on the kitchen floor, while the coffee brews and the sun pummels the air. The heat's gaining, and we're sweating like wildebeests. Achilles doesn't know that this will be the last time for a while. Once I spot Noam things are going to get difficult: I'm not the most emotionally stable person in the universe. I think at one time I might have been but life tends to curve the straight lines you walk. In my case, life's bent the lines into circles.

No, I wasn't always like this, I told Achilles once. In fact, I was a pretty normal girl.

This morning, I don't care if he or anyone else believes this or not. My heart beats twenty times faster than it should and it's not because of the fucking or the caffeine. It's because, after all these years, I'm convinced that Noam's going to contact me.

'*Battleship* tonight?' Achilles asks as he sips his café con leche.

His voice, deep and woodsy, amazes me. Achilles is a detective, though at one time he was a tenor with the Athens Opera. He says that the two are more similar than I might think. I don't really know what he means, but that's the beauty of our relationship: we have years to figure each other out. I'm just afraid that by the time I figure Achilles out, he'll already be gone.

'Maybe,' I say but he knows from the sound of my voice that he can pretty much write off this evening.

Achilles loves games. *The Game of Life, Clue, Chutes and Ladders, Monopoly.* We play them, get high, mess up the rules, strip down to our underwear. Sometimes, if we're feeling frisky, Achilles uses my breasts as an *Ouija* board. Conduits to the dead. He likes to contact his deceased grandmother, an olive-skinned woman from Patros.

'Call me later at the officio,' Achilles says.

His office, in Burbank: ACHILLES PAPPADIS, PRIVATE INVESTIGATOR.

While Achilles showers, I make him a bologna and cheese sandwich, a thermos of lemonade. I pack up his lunch and feel a growing sadness. Between here and there, between the last two years and today, I have thought of nothing but my brother. Going through the routine. I thought this might break the spell Noam's held over me. It hasn't and it's driving my Greek and me apart.

I join Achilles in the bathroom, sit on the toilet, watch him shave his beard into a goatee. The muscles of his legs clench and release, the smattering of black hairs that cover his back, downy and fine. I've never loved anyone as much as I love Achilles. Except maybe Noam.

When we first started dating, Achilles took on my case for free. He spent hours digging around. It's hard to find a trace of a ghost when the ghost doesn't want to be traced.

Once Achilles leaves, I shower and comb out what

little hair I have left. You'd think I'd be embarrassed by my appearance. Here in Los Angeles, there's a freak on every corner. This is something about Los Angeles I like. I tend to fit right in. I'm the cancer patient fighting for my life, the walking poster child for stress management. Don't let this happen to you, my eyes say. Don't let your stupid older brother ruin your life.

Today, what's left of my wavy blond hair will probably fall out altogether. Today marks the anniversary of Noam's abduction. Today marks the anniversary of my own.

Before I leave for Wax-R-Us, I grab the plastic yellow folder, which contains my statement, the police report, newspaper clippings, random sightings of Noam in Berlin and Tokyo and the last one, here, in Los Angeles, three weeks ago.

I pull into the parking lot and slide into my reserved space: Miss Bo Beep in faded white letters, with the stencil of a hooked staff in blue. I fought hard to get this space, deservedly so, since I have the furthest to walk. I began my long career as a live wax model impersonating Marilyn Monroe. When my hair started to recede, I was demoted. Being Marilyn was far too much pressure. Smile, look glamorous, speak in that inane, breathy voice. Besides, I don't really have the boobs for it.

I punch the time card, suit up, on to make up, and then it's eight hours of *Where oh where are my sheep?* I speak to kids. I say, *Have you seen my little lambs? I seem to have misplaced them* . . . and stuff like that.

My boss, Fionna, likes me a lot. She says I'm the best Bo Peep they've ever had. I guess that's saying something. I'm not an actress. I do it purely for selfish reasons.

The siren sounds, announcing the opening of the park. And it's places, places. And it's, *Is my wig on straight?* And it's, *How does my tail look?* People come to me with all of their insecurities and I tell them, *You are who you claim to be. Go out into the world and perform.*

Baa baa say the mechanical sheep.

Floods of tourists pour into Lithia Park on this sweltering summer morning. The sweat pools in the creases of my elastic waistband and these new shoes send a torturous Morse code through my nervous system. The bunion on my left foot throbs.

Missy, who plays Jayne Mansfield, parades by, her breasts so perky I want to slap her. She's from Iowa, someone all the stagehands and cowpokes go gaga over. I will never introduce her to Achilles, though she asks me about him all the time.

The sun blazes down upon us, heating up the black, wrought-iron benches, scorching the brittle yellow brick road. Dorothy, in her ruby red slippers, mutters, 'There's no place like hell,' as I move past her, into my domain of Astroturf and papier-mâché boulders. I wield my staff, gripping it with ferocity, and think about Noam. I scan the crowd, searching each face. I spritz myself with the atomizer. I take a drink of lemonade.

Baa baa go the mechanical sheep.

If only it would rain.

A week before we were leaving for Los Angeles so that my father could go on *Jeopardy!*, my mother took my brother and me to the movies. The Fox Theater sat on a parcel of land just beyond North Stall Mall. A mess of a building, faded paint and crumbling plaster, it looked more like a mausoleum in the middle of a renovation than a theatre. It'd changed management as many times over the years as my father had lost jobs. In this incarnation, the Fox was an art house, playing only classic pictures. The owner, Mr Davis, was trying to draw out the city's retirement communities, which spread across San Antonio by the hundreds.

That afternoon, there was a line full of little old ladies who shouted at one another, two middle-aged men, a couple of teenagers in black lipstick, and us, the Sikulskis.

Noam's girlfriend, my ex-best friend, Shalimar Davis, worked the concession stand. Before the Davises moved to a more tony part of town, we'd sat together on the bus, picking our enemies apart. All those years we'd been like sisters, it seemed nothing more than an elaborate smoke screen to get to my god-awful, too-handsome older brother.

Shalimar smiled that orthodontic smile at me. Half Pakistani, half English, her skin the colour of tea with milk. She always smelled of cloves from the cigarettes she smoked. Her black hair, long and luscious, fell down her back in velvety waves.

'Let's go children,' my mother said as she headed toward the door of the theatre.

'Hi, Mrs Sikulski,' Shalimar said.

'Oh, hello there,' my mother replied, cool and flat.

'Hi, Oralee,' Shalimar said to me. 'I love your skirt. Foley's right?'

'Um, not even,' I said, rolling my eyes. 'Marshall Fields.'

'I'm going to hang out here,' Noam said and planted a kiss on Shalimar's god-awful mouth.

My mother grabbed my hand and we marched off. We took seats on the far right of the theatre, my mother in the aisle.

'Oralee,' my mother said, 'just how serious is it with those two?'

'Am I my brother's keeper?' I said.

An hour later, Noam squashed down in the seat beside mine and sighed. Every once in a while, he leaned close to me as if he was about to whisper in my ear. He must have been as bored as I was. We'd both seen *Imitation of Life* about a dozen times.

At a crucial moment in the movie, Noam blurted out, 'There's a man out there in the lobby from Hollywood. He wants to give me a screen test when we're out in LA next week.'

His voice broke through me. I had no idea what he was talking about. My mother said, 'Shoosh up,' and dove her hand into the bag of popcorn Noam had brought in with him.

'But, mom,' he said.

'Don't mom me,' my mother said. 'I don't care if the Mata Hari is out there. I'm watching Lana and I don't want to hear another word out of you.'

I turned to my brother, and whispered, 'What's it for?'

Noam said, 'Some movie called *The Man Whose Face Fell Off.*'

'Tell mom it's for a movie,' I said.

'Will you two please shut up,' my mother said.

Noam got up and pushed past us, while my mother dried her eyes with a sleeve. She clutched my arm and wept until her mascara ran and snot drizzled out of her nose. As the credits rolled, we made our way toward the doors to the lobby. A sharp razor of light sliced the stained and worn carpet. As the music swelled, my mother grabbed my hand and squeezed tightly.

'Wasn't this just amazing? Just a couple more minutes,' she said.

My mother liked to take her time, reading each name aloud as if she knew each person intimately. She didn't, but in the dark, anything was possible.

In the lobby, a man in a heavy blue suit and black hat stood off to the side. He'd been speaking with Shalimar. He held a cellular phone in one hand and a clipboard in the other. A table sat behind him and a placard read, 'Auditions Today'.

'How's my baby star?' Shalimar said, throwing her arms around Noam.

'Mrs Sikulski,' the man said extending his hand. 'Noel Jenkins. RGR Studios. Um, Mrs Sikulski, I think your son is exactly what we're looking for.'

'Oh dear god,' my mother sighed.

'Expect my call, Noam,' Mr Jenkins said.

And then the four of us were in the parking lot, the sky orange to the west.

'I wonder what colour the sky is in Hollywood?' Shalimar said.

My mother turned to her and said, 'It's the same damn colour it is everywhere else.'

In the car on the way home, Noam said, 'You didn't have to say that. What's she ever done to you?'

'She's a whiny snivelling twit,' my mother said. 'And you can just forget about that screen test. It's bad enough your father's gone off the deep end with that show of his. I will not have another member of my family acting like a complete idiot. There are enough idiots in the world already.'

After lunch, my feet feel murdered. I'm sitting on a papier-mâché boulder, not really sitting but leaning because the thing's hollow and costs about $500 to replace. When I first started to work at Wax-R-Us, I didn't know this. I put my foot through three boulders in a single week.

I'm not what you'd call light on my feet. Achilles says it's because of what happened to me. He says that after that kind of experience, you and objects take on different spatial relations. Noam's the only object I'd like to relate to spatially. I'd like to tell him, See these feet? They've wandered the globe for you.

I've had plenty of retaliation fantasies. What I'd do to Noam when and if I ever found him. Because of him, my mother spiralled into one of her suicidal depressions which she never completely recovered from. My father launched a campaign against *Jeopardy!* Everybody blamed somebody else. Not me. I blamed Noam.

My nerves tingle when I think of what I'm going to do and say when I see him again. My skin itches. I feel a wonderful pressure at the base of my skull. I think about running an ice pick through Noam's tongue. I think about stabbing him in the gut with the end of my staff, which, unbeknown to anyone, I've been whittling into a spear, since the day Achilles showed me the photographs.

I pull one of these out of the yellow plastic folder. Is it Noam? I can't really tell. But if it's not Noam, then the likeness is uncanny. And all I want is to ask him is, How could you do this to us, your flesh, your bone? How could you vanish like that?

I think about my girlhood, a bad punch line to a bad joke. Yes, I blame Noam for what he did. Yes, I blame him for being a selfish, beautiful prick.

A gang of shirtless men with pierced nipples and tattoos like morning stars parade by, their chests puffed up, their little silver hoops glinting in the sunshine. Behind them, another gang and then another and I realize it must be Gay Day here at Lithia Park.

Is this what Noam has become? I wonder.

I look for him among them, these throngs of muscle-bound, steroidal men who screech and laugh, displaying an obscene amount of flesh. They wear Daisy Dukes, their legs absent of hair. Tiny volcanic craters – in-grown hairs – erupt on their shoulders and backs. If I go up to one of them and run my fingers over his skin, I know I'll feel stubble.

I think of the day Noam came into my room and asked me to shave his back. I remember the afternoon I found him standing in front of his full-length mirror in nothing but a silver mesh thong. I remember finding a lock of black hair under his pillow and thinking that it was Shalimar's.

When I first moved to Los Angeles, I trucked around in my 1974 Beetle, going from one gay bar to the next. I was looking for my brother, Cunt A. Kinte, the great white drag queen from Texas. Had anyone seen him?

'Her,' they often corrected. 'Her.'

'Yes, her then,' I said, bringing out Noam's high school yearbook picture.

Ooh and ah went the men in the bars.

'Try Hancock Park,' they told me. 'Try Lithia Park. Most dragsters get jobs there.'

I tried them both. And instead of finding Noam, I found a job as the waxy incarnation of Marilyn Monroe.

I bring out the most recent picture – thanks to Achilles – and saunter up to one of the gangs.

'Have you seen this man?' I ask.

'He's a fox,' says a man with a thick handlebar moustache toting an umbrella. 'He's gorgeous. I think I'd remember him.' The gang titters then flits away.

The man with the moustache calls after me, 'If we see

him, we'll tell him that Little Bo Peep's looking for him.'

Baa baa go the mechanical sheep.

A cloud spreads out in front of the sun, bathing the park in shadow. During my bathroom break, I call Achilles.

'Any luck?' he says.

'Not yet,' I say. 'But I'm hopeful.'

'He fucked your family,' he says. 'I just don't understand you, Oralee.'

'He's my brother,' I say. 'And I don't understand me either.'

'So no *Candyland* then,' Achilles says.

'Not tonight,' I say.

He sighs, pointedly disappointed.

After we hang up, I go into the bathroom. My face is red and chafed, my eyes swollen, my scalp oily. I stand in front of the automatic hand-dryer, angling my head so that the hot wind feathers my hair. A trick I learned from Noam.

And I wonder, as I catch myself in the mirror, Is he bald? Fat? Will I recognize him when I see him? It's been almost twenty years. I'm tired of looking for him but I can't give up. The first few years, I didn't think about him much. Back then I took care of my mother, who sat in her bedroom with the TV on, watching for her first-born child. My father was preoccupied with his strike against the TV network. And me, I spent those years trying to forget about Paladin Bob.

The sky darkens around five o'clock, two hours before I'm set to leave. I am told over the PA system: *Miss Bo Peep, in case of rain, please herd the sheep into Barn Storage Unit 3 and await further instructions.* It's only rained twice since I've been at Wax-R-Us. Thankfully, both were my days off.

The air feels eclectic and dangerous; a zipper of lightning brightens the sky to the east. Umbrellas dangle from the hands of all sorts of gay people. Gay dads, gay moms, gay teenagers. Rainbow flags fly high in the afternoon sky. The world is a rainbow.

I think of Achilles and the first time I told him about my brother.

'He played football, he bragged about all the girls he screwed,' I said, tearing up. Back then, I found it much harder to discuss Noam. Back then, I wasn't where I am right now. 'He doesn't act . . .'

Achilles said, 'So your brother sucks dick. So do you. Does that change anything?'

That was two years ago. That was right after my mother tried to kill herself for the umpteenth time and I finally had to put her in a home. Driving away from Golden Manor that day, I felt a sharp ping in my chest. I pulled onto the shoulder of the road and screamed. I couldn't speak for days. That's when I began my search in earnest for my brother. That's when I realized how debilitating and expensive grief was.

My first few months in Los Angeles, I spent a lot of time in West Hollywood, plastering Noam's picture up on message boards and telephone poles. I received many calls from crackpots in the middle of the night, lonely guys who spun incredible stories. I asked, 'Tell me three things Noam loved to do in bed,' and inevitably right after I posed this question, the line went dead.

It's not that I don't understand or can't sympathize with Noam's reasons for wanting to quit our family. I simply can't wrap my mind around the fact that he'd rather never speak to me again. This hurts most of all. And when I see him again, I'm going to tell him. I'm going to say, At least you could've taken me with you.

I'm going to scream: The first time I had sex, I was thirty-one years old.

The drops of rain fall heavy and hard across the open field. Sirens blare and thunder rebounds through the valley floor. I am told by the PA system: *Miss Bo Peep, please locate your flock and head to Barn Storage Unit 3 ASAP.* A handyman appears to remove the papier-mâché boulders.

Baa baa go the mechanical sheep.

Ooh ahh go the men I show Noam's picture to.

I'm panicked. I can't find the last sheep. I count and recount. Twelve, fifteen, twenty-six. There are twenty-seven sheep in all.

Where oh where is my last little lamb?

The rain tumbles out of the sky, heavier and harder, blackening the hills. Tiny puffs of dust are carried away by the wind. I sneeze. My eyes fill with doom. I can't afford to lose this sheep.

The barn is dry and warm with fluorescent lighting. I attach each lamb to its individual electric socket for recharge. Their eyes light up green, glowing. Their poly-synthetic-wool fur smells like wet sweaters. In the lights, they look like Chia pets.

Beyond the barn, I hear a muffled baa baa. I hear gay people squeak and squawk, the sound of umbrellas popping open, the roar of the wind blowing through Lithia Park.

I poke my head out of the door. There is the last lamb, its cloven hoof stuck in a groove in the earth. Its little head held up, the rain dashes into its unblinking eyes since sheep don't have eyelids. At least these models of sheep. It struggles to free itself as its body absorbs the rain. All of a sudden, the lamb freezes up, head stuck, mouth agape and a blue spark catches behind each eye.

I watch the lamb short-circuit. I weep as the PA system announces, *Miss Bo Peep, please see me in my office before you leave.*

At the gates to Lithia Park, we gave our names and waited as the manager escorted us inside. He handed us our complimentary tickets, which would allow us to eat completely free the entire day. 'A perk of the show,' he said. My parents waved goodbye; they were going to the studio to meet with Alex Trebek's assistant.

Characters from every animated movie lined the sidewalks, bouncing kids high into the crystal clear air. White-gloved maidens held parasols and balloons, offering pictures with anyone and everyone. I spotted Dowdy Dawg entertaining a pack of girls. They crowded around him, screaming with delight.

'I want to get my picture with Dowdy,' I said.

Noam looked at me, then over at the pack of girls.

'Aren't you a little old for that?' he said.

I put my camera away disappointedly and we headed toward Spice Mountain.

'You go ahead,' Noam said. 'I've gotta make a phone call.'

'Another one?'

'Yeah, what's it to you? I'll meet you back here in a few minutes.'

I waited in line behind a pack of boy scouts. The troop master kept close watch on them and I kind of eased my way into their group. We all seemed to be the same age and height. When it was our turn, I took a seat next to a boy whose father was related to Bob Barker. As we began our ascent into space, I looked down. Noam was standing below, reading his book, *1001 Monologues to Instantaneous Fame.*

When we were safely back on the ground, I exited feeling a little lightheaded. Noam was waiting for me at the exit, the book still in his hands.

'Oralee, about the Dowdy thing . . . I'm just a little nervous about this screen test,' he said.

'Oh dear god,' I said.

'That guy from RGR studios. I'm meeting him at Lunar Landing around three o'clock.'

Noam looked up at Spice Mountain and began to recite his monologue: 'You come here and sprinkle the place with powder and spray perfume and cover the light bulb with a paper lantern, and lo and behold the place has turned into Egypt and you are Queen of the Nile! Sitting on your throne and swilling down my liquor!'

When he finished, he slapped the book against his thigh and said, 'That part's as good as mine.'

At half-past three, we were idling in front of Lunar Landing eating cotton candy, when a heavy-set man in a three-piece suit approached us.

'Well, shall we go?' he said, taking out his cellular phone.

'Sure,' Noam said and turning to me, 'You gonna be okay for a while?'

I nodded my head. I was eleven years old. Why wouldn't I be okay?

The two of them walked away, Noam clutching his book, the man speaking rapidly to someone on his phone. The sun was hot and the air thick with smog. I coughed and sneezed. I sat down on a bench beside a man dressed in a dark-green uniform. I sneezed again and a tissue dangled in front of my face. I blew my nose.

'My allergies act up real bad this time of year,' he said. 'You lost or something?'

'No, I'm waiting for my brother,' I said.

A burst of static filled the air around us as he reached for his walkie-talkie. 'Paladin Bob here,' he said, smiling and rolling his eyes. 'Yup, yup. Right. I'm on it.' He stuffed the walkie-talkie back into his pocket. Then, he said, 'You want to escort me to the Haunted Hotel?'

This was supposed to be my day, I heard myself telling Paladin Bob as I followed him to a shady, secluded spot around the side of the Haunted Hotel.

'My brother's a jerk too,' Bob said. 'Most people are.'

I looked at Bob, at the lines around his eyes. He was old and balding.

'We're on vacation,' I said. 'My father's a contestant on *Jeopardy!* And if he wins, we're going to be here at least another two weeks. My brother, he's at an audition for some movie. He wants to be an actor and move to Los Angeles but my mother won't let him.'

Bob leaned into me. He sniffed my hair. He touched my chin with the tip of his index finger. It wasn't creepy. Sort of sad is all.

'I've been out here for years. Came to act,' Bob said. 'Well, this is a tough place. Not for everyone.'

'Noam wants to be an actor more than anything in the world. His girlfriend, Shalimar, she used to be my best friend, I think they're probably going to get married one day. I hate her. She's a real bitch,' I said.

'You have a special someone back home?' Bob said.

'Not really. I don't really understand boys,' I said.

'I know what boys want,' he said softly. 'They want to hold you all night and run their fingers through your pretty hair. They want to whisper sweet things into your ear and buy you caramels.'

'That's not true,' I said. 'The boys I know, all they

want to do is touch my boobies and then brag about it to their friends.'

'Well, maybe you need someone a little older,' Bob said, smiling.

Another burst of static filled the air around us. I thought about my mother and father, about what I would tell them when they came to pick us up. I thought about Noam and my stomach somersaulted. What if I missed him? What if he was waiting for me right now?

'I, I have to go,' I said.

'Me too,' he said. 'King Kong fell over and crushed a little old lady. Damage control, that's me. Paladin Bob to the rescue.' He pretended to shoot an arrow into the air.

I pulled a rubber band out of my Hello Kitty purse and tied my hair in a ponytail. Paladin Bob escorted me back to the bench. The bell tower in the distance rang six times; we were supposed to meet our parents at the gates.

Bob said, 'This is my beeper number,' and handed me a scrap of paper. 'If you need anything, anything at all, young lady, don't hesitate to call on Paladin Bob.'

And then just like that, he moved away.

I sat down on the bench, fanning myself a little with my hands. The viscous heat sank around me, molten and unreal. I wondered if Noam was already at the gates but something told me he wasn't. I saw him being offered ice-cold sodas and Snickers bars and Doritos. Families wandered past me, swinging arms and pink clouds of cotton candy.

I got up and followed them to the entrance.

The sun makes an appearance after the rain ceases, boiling the moisture in the air. It's impossible to breathe normally. I catch little snippets of oxygen from the EORT, the Emergency Oxygen Reservoir Tank, hanging on the wall of the barn.

The sheep say nothing.

Replacing my police report, dog-eared and thin as parchment, the PA system announces the five o'clock performance of Dizzy the Dolphin.

Before I leave for the day, I brush each sheep with a special demagnetized comb and spray its wool with Growth Hormone D-876. This gives their coats a healthy sheen. In two weeks, it's Wool Harvest Season. It's in my contract to see that my little lambs remain in their pristine states.

I wander past Artificial Mammal 27, AM-27 for short; and into the main building to see Fionna.

I wait in Arbitration Room F. F for fuck me. F for fare thee well. F for Fionna who slides into the room, rearranges her helmet of black hair, which has been disassembled in the journey from her office some thirty-eight stories above. A drop of blood clings to her right nostril; a side effect of the mach elevator. There are other side effects, like dizziness and cramping, but we take pills for these. Fionna pops a blue pill, tilts her head back, swallows.

She wobbles unsteadily to the table and sits down hard in the chair opposite mine. I hand her the Facex tissue I've been clutching for the last half an hour, and say, 'Side Effect 9.' Because of their material, the tissues are washable. Blood, however, will take me days of soaking.

Immediately, Fionna dabs at her nose, says, 'Oralee, I feel your pain,' and blows into the tissue. It turns a deep, dark red. 'Jesus, we really need to upgrade those damn elevators. This is the sixth Side Effect 9 in three weeks.'

Out the porthole window, gay kids perch on their gay dads' shoulders, waving little rainbow flags. Some wear *I Dove With Dizzy* T-shirts. Some clutch shiny pennies in their palms.

Fionna says, 'Under article twelve, subheading eight, clause sixteen point two of the "Thou Shalt Not" contract you signed back in August, parties of the first part – that's me – shall assign and conscript damages to parties of the second part – that's you – should any unforeseen problems arise. Unforeseen problems have arisen.' She pauses to dab at her nose again. 'What happened out there today?'

I watch gay moms in their rainbow flag tube tops suck down rainbow-coloured spumoni as night descends on Lithia Park. And Fionna tells me that I owe $7,203.97. 'Parts and labour', she adds.

I want to tell her the story of my brother. It would help to explain where I've been the last couple of years. It would help explain why my hair's falling out, why I can't sleep, why I'm nearly bankrupt, emotionally, financially. Why Achilles's touch sometimes feels like an infection. Why I wake up screaming in the middle of the night with Paladin Bob on my lips.

I say, 'It wasn't my fault. That sheep went AWOL. That little lamb malfunctioned. I can't be responsible for everyone's damn happiness, Fionna.'

'It's fully operational this morning,' she says. 'Our sheep don't just break down. Our sheep are state-of-the-art technology. They're designed to outlast the pyramids.'

Fionna misses the fact that it took thousands of slaves to erect those pyramids. That they didn't have much of a choice. Build or die, that was about it. What Fionna doesn't realize is that I'm alive, the sheep aren't. They never were.

'Are we finished here?' I say. 'Are we?'

'I don't know, Oralee,' she says, her voice pinched and cold. 'You tell me. You tell me what to do.'

'I'd like a transfer,' I say. 'I'd like to work with Dizzy.'

Fionna shuffles her stack of papers on the table, smoothing their edges down before replacing them in the hermetically sealed envelope. She rises, walks toward the elevator.

'I'll see what I can do,' she says. 'In the meantime, I'd like you to sign up for one of my "Re-upload and Revival" seminars. And between you and me, Oralee, it's time to start the Propecia treatments.'

Entering the elevator, Fionna is whisked from the room. Out the porthole window, the sky darkens and the firefly-shaped lamps flicker on. For a second, and only for that long, I think I spot Noam, his long, carved face, his bangles and bulk. I tap on the porthole's glass with my fist, calling his name. I rifle through the pictures Achilles gave me. He's in a bar in Echo Park, a dance club in Silver Lake, he's lifting weights in West Hollywood. He looks like every other homosexual, the same eyes, the same tattoo, the same magazine-perfect body.

I rush out into the evening, down the brittle yellow brick road, around Little Lost Lamb Meadow. Except for its severed hoof, AM-27 has been removed. The air smells miserable. Up and down, through the gay gangs, which continue to pour into Lithia Park, I search for my brother. I clutch his picture in my hand, Noam, the mad sassy drag queen from San Antonio.

The moon ripens, full and bright, as I make my way toward the entrance of Lithia Park. The park will stay open all night and come morning, most of these men, alone or in pairs, will get back into their cars and drive home. They will leave behind a trail of tiny amber-glass bottles of amyl nitrate and empty thumbnail-sized baggies of Special K. In the morning, I will find used condoms in the meadow. Some of my sheep will have been sodomized.

On the third morning after Noam's disappearance, the police came to the hotel. They took my parents into a small room to ask them questions. They told them Noam had not been abducted. That no signs of foul play were in evidence. He had simply vanished. Based on what we told them, they cited possible places he could have gone: a bar for boys who sold themselves for money; and Hancock Park, a place known for soliciting with intent. They threw the word hustler around.

My mother locked herself in the broom closet with a pint of gin. My father studied furiously, not stopping to eat or sleep. He refused to do anything about the police's allegations until he was done with *Jeopardy!*

'My brother's going to be a movie star,' I told the police proudly. 'Doesn't that mean anything?'

'Out here, kid,' the police said, 'everyone's a star.'

During all of this, *Jeopardy!* called to tell my father that Alex Trebek was feeling better – he'd had a case of the stomach flu – and they'd like to begin taping as soon as possible. My parents were torn: my mother wanted to stay at the hotel, my father wanted to go to the studio. My mother caved in and decided to go to the studio with my father. 'For moral support', she said. And me, I was to wait at the hotel, just in case Noam showed up.

Alone in the room, I was watching TV when someone

knocked on the door. I was sure it was Noam, but when I opened the door, there was Paladin Bob. He didn't say anything as he moved quietly into the room. He wore neither his dark-green uniform nor his nametag. His face shined oily and tan.

'You alone?' he said.

'Yeah, they went to the studio in Burbank. Today's the big day,' I said.

'I guess you're wondering what I'm doing here,' he said. He seemed eager and forlorn. 'Um, it's sort of hard to explain.' He paused and went to the window. 'Wanna go for a drive with me?'

I said, 'I can't leave. What if Noam comes back?'

'That's sort of why I'm here . . .' he said.

'What?' I said. 'You know where my brother is?'

'Do you wanna go or not?' Bob said.

I stared at the TV, hearing the world in minor chords, the music on the TV, the chug of the diesel trucks. Dusk settled on Los Angeles. The lights of the industrial park, the highway, the strange orange glow on the horizon. I thought about Noam, the hours he spent in the bath-room. About the afternoon I finally realized it wasn't a lock of Shalimar's hair under his pillow but Darius's, her brother.

We pulled out of the hotel's parking lot. Bob gripped the wheel tightly, his fingers thick as tree roots. He hummed along with the radio, rocking his head.

'Do you know where Noam is?' I said at last.

Los Angeles erupted on all sides, billboards and crazy kids hanging out on the street, palm trees, liquor stores, one strip mall after the other.

'Sunset Boulevard,' Bob said, pressing his hand against his window. 'And that's Duke's. It's where all the producers have breakfast. I've sat in there a thousand times waiting for someone to notice me. No one ever does. The fuckers.'

Out my window, brightly lit movie theatres and coffee shops. It all seemed pleasant enough from where I was sitting, safe in the world of Bob's yellow Impala.

'Hollywood Boulevard, Street of Broken Dreams. When I first got here, back in '62, this street was nothing but hustlers and prostitutes, starlets looking to make it big . . . Lana Turner used to walk this street, hunting for her next meal. She slept many a night in one flea trap or another. Jayne Mansfield was decapitated, did you know that? But that was a long time ago. Look at it now,' Bob said, tsking as though he and Jayne had been best friends.

We stopped at a light and Bob leaned into me, his hand finding its way to my thigh.

'I missed you,' he said. 'Whaddya think about that?'

He kneaded the skin through my dungarees. A warm gift on this cold summer night. I let him leave it.

'You don't know anything about Noam, do you?' I said.

His eyes left the street for a moment as he contemplated my question.

'Of course I do,' he said. 'I don't lie.'

We came to another cluster of traffic lights, the last along this stretch of Hollywood Boulevard. The street was choked with rundown motels, red signs with $16 PER NIGHT flashing in the windows. Bob pulled over to the curb and parked. Men and women huddled together in darkened doorways, their faces pulled into tight grins. Girls my age in gaudy sundresses, faces painted like clowns, lingered at the curb, while policemen trolled up and down. I watched them, wondering if anyone would ask what I was doing with this ugly, lonely, fifty-year-old man.

I climbed out of the car. A patrolman spoke into his radio, a girl with a bloodied eye smoked in the back-seat. Her lips matched the colour of the cigarette's tip. I slipped quietly beside Paladin Bob and, together, we walked through the doors of the motel.

No one uttered a word.

I drive down Santa Monica Boulevard, which has been torn up for years. This part of West Hollywood is hideous. But it's the most likely place to spot Noam. I'm drawn into this decadence, where men have sex in the shadows and the music goes on all night. I find the bars comforting, the men friendly. I buy them vodka tonics and they smooth out the wrinkles in my skirt.

I want to tell them that when I finally find Noam, I'm going to murder him. About my mother who swears she sees Noam in the trees outside her window. About Paladin Bob and what he said to me that night: that I was too ugly to fuck. That he saw Noam and his heart had been snatched away. Sometimes, I even look around for Paladin Bob.

Because traffic is absurd and parking terrible, I drive right past the bars tonight, past tiny cafes where men sit outside, biceps flexing as they raise their wineglasses. Their eyes, caught in my headlights, are glassy as deers'. I make two loops up and down Santa Monica, pull up to a group of men in spandex tops.

I say, 'Have you seen this man?' and slide a picture through the window.

'Isn't that Cunt A.?' one of them asks.

'He's my brother,' I say through the window.

'She,' they say. 'She.'

'Listen here, Heidi,' says a sickly looking man. He leans his drunken face into the car. 'Cunt A.'s performing tonight around two o'clock at Club Fuck in Pasadena. You an agent or something?'

Pasadena. That's miles and miles away.

'Are you positive?' I say.

'No, but I just got over hepatitis B,' he says. 'Why?'

I drive away, leaving the picture, the men, the incessant throb of Santa Monica Boulevard behind. It's late, I'm tired, and the thought of confronting Noam fills me with dread. I'm just his sister, someone who used to pluck his eyebrows and wax his legs. I'm just another he left behind.

I have hours before Noam goes on at Club Fuck so I drive home. In the parking lot of our building, I stare up at the window of our apartment. Blue light spills out of the TV and I know that Achilles is playing *The Game of Life* by himself. He spins the wheel, moves his piece around the board.

I pull out of the lot, letting my imagination take me back to a more promising time. When my father won enough money on *Jeopardy!* to buy my mother a new car, when I took a picture with Dowdy Dawg, and stayed in the same motel where Lana Turner had slept. When Paladin Bob taught me the secret of boys: no matter how nice you are, they will always leave.

At Mann's Chinese Theater on Hollywood Boulevard, I buy a ticket for whichever show's playing. In two hours, it will be midnight and I'll drive to Pasadena. I will sit in the audience and watch my bitch of a brother lip-synch. Then, I'll go backstage and punch him in the gut. While he's doubled over, I'll tell him, Love doesn't grow on trees, Noam. I'll tell him, People are more important than fame.

In the theatre, the lights dim, the music soars. I've seen this movie before, a long time ago in some other city. I already know how it ends. Sometimes, the only surprise is that there isn't one. I sink into the darkness, eleven years old again, and eat my popcorn.

# quite cold in alaska

After a ten-hour flight, which should've only taken three,
a rumpled and hungry Damon Fein stood at the counter
of ReadySetGone Rent-a-car. The clerk's face, tan and
wrinkle-free, like polyester, Damon thought. He took
him immediately for a homosexual – the soft-patterned
speech, the pastel-blue shirt, the tiny rainbow flag
pinned to his lapel – and removed his sun-glasses with a
stealthy intent. He took a tiny hop closer to the counter,
leaning in. He waited, as he normally did, for the recog-
nition in the clerk's face, that second of OH WOW.
You could rob the world with those eyes, Suzanne had
once told him. And Damon believed her. It was the
nicest thing she'd ever said to him.

'Let me see what I can do,' the clerk said warmly and
disappeared with Damon's fax into the back.

Damon sighed with relief. A snap, he thought.
Through the dusty, tinted windows, a plane shivered
into the sky, the late-morning sun bouncing off the silver
wings. Damon thought about Suzanne's last layover in
Dallas when she'd told him, 'I love you, Damon, but I
just can't marry you. You're a child and I'm not your

mother.' Then, a few hours later, her plane had vanished mysteriously somewhere over the Atlantic Ocean.

'Sir, I'm sorry,' the clerk said. 'This won't do. In the state of California, you must have a current driver's licence to rent a car.'

Perhaps because he was slightly drunk, Damon leaned across the yellow-speckled counter and said, quietly, 'You. Fucking. Faggot.'

'What was that?' the clerk said, glaring up at him from his computer screen, eyes twisted behind a pair of glasses.

'It's just a car, not an atomic submarine, man,' he said and cracked a guilty smile.

'NEXT', the clerk said.

Outside, Damon walked in circles around a giant potted palm, wondering what to do. It was approaching noon. He thought sadly, If Suzanne were here, and walked back into the store to use the payphones.

When West answered, Damon said, 'I thought you said everyone out here's friendly.'

A pause, 'Who's this?'

'The Daily Llama,' he said.

West didn't laugh. 'You're late,' he said.

'You saw that in your crystal ball?' he said.

'Mom was at it again this morning,' his younger brother said.

'The Wandering Jewess,' he said.

'That's not funny, Damon,' West said but he could tell that West was grinning. 'So I'm not that far away. Catch a cab. And Damon, I'm glad you're here.'

Damon climbed the long, steep stairs that led to his brother's house in the Hollywood Hills. He heard his family. His mother's crackling laughter, his father's hard, incessant sssh's. He was always shushing her. Why did I agree to this? he thought as he took a deep breath and walked through the creaking wooden gate.

'Damon,' his mother, Mae, said, 'We thought you probably got lost. But there you are!'

She hugged him close. She felt frailer in his arms than the last time he'd seen her at Thanksgiving. Her black hair, gone completely grey, was tinted a terrible, bright red, which matched her nail polish and lipstick. Damon turned to his father to avoid Mae's eyes.

'Hiya, pop,' he said.

Sitting in a lounge chair that swallowed him up, his father grinned.

'To what do we owe this unexpected pleasure?' he half said, half sneered.

'Larry,' Mae said, 'please.'

West came out of the house carrying a large tray of ice teas. Even from where he stood, Damon smelled the rum. Long Island iced teas. West set the tray down on the table and said, 'What's with the car, Damon?'

He couldn't say that he'd lost his wallet. He couldn't say that in the last four months, he could barely stretch his arm to the telephone which sat by the bed. He shrugged.

'I'll take care of it when we get back,' he said. 'Right now, I think I'd like to take a shower. Show me where it is, little brother.'

While his parents sipped their cocktails and bickered over the itinerary, Damon followed West up the stairs to his room. 'Dude, this is . . . majestic,' he said, flopping down on the white bedspread, laying his face in the cool white pillows. 'I'm going to sleep like a horse.'

The brilliant afternoon sun poured into the room, through the French doors that led out to the small balcony. In the distance, Damon caught the Hollywood sign, its white letters set in stark relief against the darker shade of the trees. West disappeared into the bathroom and came out clutching a couple of towels.

'Mom and pop look old,' he said, shifting around on the bed to face his brother.

'That's what people do,' West said, appraising Damon. 'They get old.'

'Not all people,' he said.

The two studied each other, a strange distance overtaking them. 'Are you sure you want to go through with this?' his brother said.

Rising, he went out on the balcony. An ashtray, some kind of seashell, pink and sparkling, sat on the railing, full of water and half-finished butts. It reeked of tar and nicotine.

'No, I'm not,' he said as West, his successful screenwriting brother, took a spot next to him. He lit a cigarette and handed it to Damon.

'Me neither,' West said.

'It won't be that bad,' Damon offered, his voice making it sound more like a question. 'Besides, we're not paying for it. We might as well enjoy the ride.'

West nodded. 'Matthew's meeting us halfway,' he said. 'I haven't mentioned it again to mom and dad.'

They all knew about West's 'friend' Matthew, though no one had ever met him. He seemed a circumstantial ghost in West's life, never there but always present.

'Don't tell them until we're on the road,' Damon said. 'Keep the worrying to a minimum.'

'You don't mind if he meets us, do you?' West said.

'West,' Damon said, 'what's to mind?'


Damon stood out on the balcony, smoking a joint. That's what he did when he couldn't sleep. It had been

Suzanne's constant worry that Damon would end up in jail eventually and he thought about this as he took another puff. He hadn't started smoking again until a few weeks after the black box had been recovered from flight 493. He used to tell Suzanne, I'm a dealer, not a user. Now, Damon smoked nearly every day, sometimes three, four times.

Below him, he listened to the sound of Los Angeles, its whirring traffic, the faint rush of the ocean. He knew that it was impossible to hear the ocean from where he was but he liked to think that it was that close.

'Damn ocean,' he said, stubbing out the joint. He wanted to spit into it.

His head felt woozy and light, detached. He drifted inside, and down the stairs. There, he found Mae stationed at the front door. She was dressed in the same clothes she'd had on that morning. She clutched her pocketbook under her arm.

'Mom,' Damon said, pressing his hands against her shoulders.

'My children are taking me on a lovely trip up the coast,' she said.

'That's right, mom,' Damon said. He wondered if she could smell the smoke on him. 'But that's not until tomorrow.'

'Will Suzanne be joining us?' she said. 'She's such a nice girl.'

'No, mom,' Damon said. 'No Suzanne this time. But we're going to meet West's friend, Matthew. Won't that be fun?'

She turned to face him. Damon felt suddenly like a little boy again, lost in the grocery store. Mae reached into her pocketbook and extracted a picture. West and

Damon as kids dressed up in cowboy hats and denim shirts.

'I'm worried about Damon, my oldest,' she said. 'He doesn't visit me anymore. Do you know why?'

'He's been very busy,' he said. 'But it has nothing to do with you. He wanted me to tell you that.'

He led Mae upstairs to his parents' bedroom. His father snored behind the door.

'I don't think he likes his father very much,' she whispered. 'I don't really like him very much either.' She smiled. 'But we've been married for forty-two years.'

'Goodnight, mom,' Damon said and kissed her gently on the forehead. Then, he went into the kitchen to fix himself a meatloaf sandwich.


With the sun not yet risen, the Feins piled into the four-door Taurus and left the city of Los Angeles. Larry drove and West sat beside him; Damon sat in the back with Mae. They drifted up the coast on that beautiful spring morning, the spray of the sea astounding him.

'Unbelievable,' Damon said. And tried not to think of his trip with Suzanne to the island of Rhodes. A name he'd always remember because it was Suzanne's surname. A different sea, the Aegean, crystal green water and pure white beaches. The dark black of the Pacific seemed oily and hard, uninviting.

'Honey, did you hear me?' Mae said, touching his shoulder. He flinched. 'I was telling you about nana's pelvis. The doctors seem to think that it's not related to the lung cancer at all. They think she just, well, sat down funny on the toilet.'

'Jesus, Mae,' Larry said. 'This is our vacation for God's sake. I thought we said we wouldn't mention your mother's broken anything.'

'Well, Larry,' Mae said, dourly, 'I was just updating them.'

'Then, maybe we should stop and call her? Maybe I should let you out and you can catch a bus back to Fort Worth,' Larry said.

They stopped to take in a scenic view at Big Sur. While their parents drifted down to the promontory, the white waves crashing against the black jetties, Damon turned to West and said, 'Do you think we should tell her that nana's dead?'

West said, 'Does it matter?'

Larry and Mae shuffled up in their brightly coloured jogging suits. Damon looked at this pair celebrating their forty-third anniversary. He looked at West, the thriving writer, who'd sprung for his ticket out to California. He thought of West's house and how much he'd paid for it. ('Something like $800,000,' Larry had whispered to him that morning.) Then, he thought of Matthew, flying in from wherever he'd been to meet them in Monterey.

Mae went to the car and returned with the camera. Larry, West, and Damon were discussing West's latest writing project with Miramax.

'Jesus,' Larry said. 'You hear that Mae? This kid's got something.' He laughed. 'You think you got a part for your old man? Sean Connery's got nothing on me.' He laughed again.

'Maybe there's a part in it for Damon,' Mae said eagerly.

'Mom,' Damon said, 'I haven't acted in years.'

Larry said, 'You had real promise.'

'I'll look into it,' West said and winked at Damon.

'Say kunk,' Mae said, aiming her camera at the three men. (Kunk, Damon's childhood word for skunk.)

'Kunk,' they said in unison.

'Anyone need the bathroom before we head out?' Larry said.

Damon sat down on the cold plastic seat. Six more days, he thought, flushing. West came in as he splashed ice cold water over his face.

'They're just happy to see you is all,' West said.

'You got any weed?' Damon asked, over the buzz of the hand dryer.

West zipped up and at the door, said, 'That stuff gives me angina. But I got just the thing you need.' He handed him a tiny pill with a triangle cut out of its centre.

'Valium, my love,' he said, looking at the pill, which seemed like a yellow button off someone's shirt. 'I'm about to lose it.'

'Lose it later,' West said.

'I shouldn't have come,' he said.

'Don't make me beat you senseless,' West said, smiling.

'Do you really think you could get me a part?' Damon asked.

'Do you really think I'm writing a screenplay for Miramax?' he said.

The Valium's effect on Damon, though insubstantial, bought him a couple of hours of sleep. When he woke up, bellboys were pulling their luggage from the trunk.

'Good morning, sleepy head,' Mae said.

A Diet Coke sat in her lap and she offered it to Damon. His mouth hurt, as if he'd been punched. Outside the car, dusk had settled over the strange hilly landscape. Random lights blinked on and off.

'These Mexican bastards,' Larry said, 'you tell them one thing, they do something else. Easy there, muchachos!' He followed the luggage into the hotel, panting.

Damon stared after his father, a despair cracking wide open. Is this what I have to look forward to? he thought. Screaming at people who don't understand a word I'm saying anyway?

Though he would never admit it, he'd always felt more akin to these sorts of guys than the college-bound guys he'd hung around with in high school. Something about them, the way they laboured, the way they stood, their shoulders back, as if pride weren't learned but something they'd been born with. Damon realized he had very little pride. Suzanne was the only person who knew this about him.

When they'd met on a flight from Cincinnati, she'd said, 'I'm not the kind of girl who needs a fancy house or three automobiles or a trip to Paris.' And that is how they had lived – for three years. No cars, no houses, no trips to Paris or anywhere else. By the end, her voice had become a shrill wind through their rented one-bedroom apartment.

Damon, Mae and West lingered at the front desk, waiting for Larry. West studied himself in the mirror behind the desk, Mae flipped through a book of coupons.

'Your father doesn't like it when I do this but,' she said, 'what he doesn't know won't hurt him.'

She handed the coupon to the girl behind the counter who took it and fiddled with the computer.

'You're all set, Mrs Fein,' she said. 'One suite, a fold-out sofa and a cot.'

Damon fell into the couch against the wall. West sat down beside him.

He said, 'They've got a pool at least.'

'This place is awful,' Damon said, looking around him. 'It's not like they don't have enough money. I mean, this is nothing better than a Motel 6.'

West rose and walked outside to speak to Larry, who was battling with the attendant over the car. Every once in a while, they would turn their bodies away from the window and nod their heads.

'Darling, come up to the room with me,' Mae said.

The room, with its orange shag carpet and avocado-green chintz curtains, shrieked early 1970s. The spread on the king-size bed was covered in swimming, geometric designs and made Damon dizzy. He found it amusing that if he'd been stoned, he probably would have been able to stare at the bedspread for hours.

He pressed a hand against the cool window, wishing it opened but it didn't. A television, a ratty sofa, a single, mottled dresser with a complimentary basket of fruit. The room held its warm, stale breath, as if it hadn't been aired out in ages.

'Who's Matthew?' she said.

Damon turned to her. Her fiery red hair seemed absurdly artificial in the glow of the room's overhead light. She tapped her nails against the bed.

'A friend of West's,' Damon said.

'I remember so little these days,' Mae said from the bed, sighing. 'Sometimes, I wake up in the middle of the night and wonder what this old man is doing in my bed. Then I see my own hands and I know. It's terrible.'

'You're fine, mom,' Damon said and took his hand off the glass. But she wasn't fine and everyone knew it. This is going to be Mae's last trip for a while, he thought.

Larry and West burst through the door, dragging the luggage. Larry's face was full of sweat. It dripped off his ears and rolled off his nose.

'The idiots took it to the wrong room, Mae,' he said. 'What's wrong with this state? Why in the hell do you live here, West?'

He simply said, 'I like the weather,' and left it at that.

'Here we are,' Larry said, closing the door behind him.

'I'm going to . . . um, get the cot,' Damon said.

Larry stood in front of the door. 'I'm glad you could make it,' he said and touched Damon on the shoulder.

'Don't,' Damon said and rushed around Larry. 'I'll be back in a while.'

Damon wandered from floor to floor, each one exactly like the other. He hadn't been inside a hotel since the last time he and Suzanne had been in downtown Dallas; a surprise weekend getaway. He'd paid for the weekend himself, having sold off the rest of his stash. They'd stayed at a four-star bed and breakfast, lounged by the pool, ate room service every night. And then, when they were driving back to Irving, a suburb, he'd asked her to marry him.

Damon went to the front desk, where a youngish woman in a white blouse sat staring at her computer screen.

'The cot,' he began, 'for room 759?'

She looked up, her eyes bloodshot as if she'd been crying. She hit a button on the computer.

'I'm afraid we're all out of cots,' she said. 'That room comes with a sofa-bed. Just give it a good tug. It's much more comfortable than a cot by the by.'

'But there are four of us,' Damon said.

'Oh,' she said. It seemed to Damon that she was having a hard time. She tapped on the keyboard, pressed another button, spoke to someone on the phone. 'Everything's full-up because of that convention.'

Her voice was thick and unlived, like glue. Damon sniffed the air and for a moment, got the faintest whiff of smoke riffling off her. He smiled. She's high as a kite, he thought.

'You don't by any chance have room service?' Damon said. He'd already gotten past the idea that he would have to sleep on the floor.

Nearly giggling, she said, 'Well, that's an idea. But no, I'm afraid not. However, there is a wonderful place just down the road on the opposite side of the highway. Amazing Angus steaks. Good beer. Great bar, too. Fantastic ambience, if ambience is what you're after.'

'Yes, ambience,' he said. 'Thank you. I'm Damon, by the way.' He paused. 'And I'm not with the convention,' he added and felt stupid afterward.

'Lilly,' she said. 'Wade's a friend of mine. I'll make a reservation for you.'

'Wonderful,' he said. 'Um, this may sound strange but I was just wondering if there was a place to, well, to buy –'

Lilly said, 'Meet me at the pool,' and smiled. She had great gaps between her teeth, her nose was crooked, her eyes too narrow. Even so, Damon found something appealing about her.

He made his way outside to the empty pool and sat down in one of the lounge chairs. It was a cool night, the air full of chlorine and steam. The highway spun out in a thin black line. The occasional truck rumbled by. As he waited for Lilly, he thought about Suzanne. He wondered if she'd felt any pain, if the plane had exploded or if she'd screamed. He thought about the statistical chances of a plane crash.

At any given moment, six thousand planes are flying around up there, Suzanne had told him once while they were lying in bed. It's perfectly safe. Besides, I love my job and I get to see the world for free.

Lilly appeared on the opposite side of the pool. She wore a blue sweater now which hid her lumpy body. Damon couldn't help wondering what she looked like undressed. He preferred plump women to thin, mainly because plump women's standards were lower. She ducked under a looming palm tree, her face momentarily exposed by the match's flame. She waved him over and he rose quickly, magnetized.

He took the joint from Lilly, said, 'Cheers,' and drew on it. His usual practice was to close his eyes but he left them open, taking in Lilly, the palm tree, the pink stucco walls of the hotel. Lilly said, 'There's not much else to do around here,' and blew out a ring of smoke. 'But it's peaceful and folks are nice.'

'My first time,' Damon said, head fuzzing up. 'Never been to California before.'

'Originally, I'm from Boston,' Lilly said, rocking a little. 'I moved out here to be with a guy.'

She looked off in the distance, as if the guy in question were making his way toward them. She offered no further explanation.

'Well, welcome to San Luis Obispo,' Lilly said, slipping him an extra joint and went back into the hotel.

Damon returned to his lounge chair. He shut his eyes, listening to the soft lap of the pool, the wind in the palms. He was pleasantly stoned and he sat for a while, dozing. It was only after his stomach grumbled that he got up to tell his family about the reservation at Angry Wade's.

West was in the hallway on his cellphone. He said, rather indignantly, 'They're *supposed* to be black.'

He went inside. Someone had drawn the curtains and because of it, the room seemed much smaller. It smelled of rubbing alcohol and Ben Gay. A familiar feeling had come over the furniture. Larry came out of the bathroom. His forehead was wet and he looked pale. His brown eyes, Damon's eyes, were distant and troubled. For a second, Damon wanted to go to him. Instead, he went to the window and said, 'I found us some Angus beef.'

Mae looked up from her toes and said, 'Is it a Sizzler, Damon? What kind of place is it?'

'How should he know?' Larry said. 'It's not like he lives here.'

Mae said, lightheartedly, 'I don't live in Alaska but I can sure imagine that it must be cold in the winter.'

'Well, then, let's get this over with,' Larry said and walked out of the room.

At the door, Mae said, 'You know how your father gets when he's hungry.'

He'd heard this rationale his entire life. But now, Mae's words were simply sad and defensive. The saddest thing of all, Damon thought, was that Mae herself accepted the excuse.

West snapped his phone shut and then the four were in the elevator. Larry seemed scrawnier to Damon all of a sudden, lesser and balder and more helpless. The Budweiser belt buckle cut into his gut, which rode up and over the waistline of his Wrangler jeans. Beside him, Damon stood an inch or two taller, and wondered how it was he'd ever felt threatened by him.

In the car, he sat up front with Larry, guiding him to Angry Wade's.

'Take a left, pop,' he said, 'under the highway.'

In daylight, Larry liked to speed. His shaky hands on the wheel that night told Damon an entirely different story. Here's a man falling into old age, he thought. A man whose wife doesn't remember him from one day to the next. A man who's stayed married merely out of convenience.

And he remembered the conversation nearly twenty years before when he'd asked his father if he was still in love with his mother.

'Love,' Larry had said. 'What's love? Your mother and I get along. We're compatible. Besides, I had no idea that when I married her she was going to be an heiress.'

Larry parked the car and sat there, sweating, breathing heavily. He wiped his forehead with a handkerchief.

'You did fine,' Mae said.

'Of course I did,' Larry said. 'I can drive, been doing it my whole life.'

'Dad, mom wasn't attacking you,' West said.

'Don't you start in on me too,' Larry said, shutting off the engine. 'I don't need your lip. Not tonight. Not on my vacation.'

Angry Wade's was dark with heavy wood panelling. Hams hung from the ceiling and the smell of hickory smoke, thick and savoury, stung Damon's eyes. They were seated immediately.

'It never fails,' Larry said. 'There're a dozen empty tables and the morons insist on seating us in the middle.'

'Would you like to move, dear?' Mae said, sipping her Long Island iced tea.

Larry said, 'I'll make do. It's not the end of the world.'

Waiters and waitresses swam by, carrying sizzling platters of meat. The Feins ordered quickly and while they waited for their food, West said, 'I guess now's the best time to remind you guys: My friend Matthew's meeting us in Monterey.'

Larry looked at Damon and somehow, he knew that he'd be blamed for this, his brother's importunity.

Larry leaned back in his seat, hands behind his head. He said, 'This Matthew character's meeting us in Monterey?'

'Dad, I told mom on the phone that he was coming,' West said. 'I said that Matthew just finished shooting –'

'Your mother doesn't remember,' Larry said.

Mae's eyes were stationed on something beyond the windows of the restaurant.

'Well, it's just going be a treat to meet your friend,' she said at last to West. 'It's true that I don't remember you telling us that he was coming but that's all right. It's all right, Larry.'

Larry brought his hands down on the armrests of his chair.

'Did you know about this little plan of your brother's?' he said to Damon.

Damon said tentatively, 'Sure.'

'I see,' Larry said. 'Well, let me break this to all of you. This is my vacation and on my vacation, there aren't going to be any tagalongs or – variations. Is that clear?' The food arrived during Larry's speech but he kept on anyway. 'And in case this isn't satisfactory with some people at this table, those people can just catch a bus back to wherever the devil takes them. In fact, I'll spring for the ticket.' He reached for his wallet.

At one point, West pushed himself away from the table. Damon thought he was going to get up and leave the restaurant and he said quickly, 'Let's just eat our dinner and discuss this later.'

'That's a marvellous idea,' Mae said. 'Let's eat our dinner and discuss this later.'

'There's nothing to discuss,' Larry said. 'I have no desire to meet any of your friends, West.'

West folded in upon himself, stuffing his mouth with a piece of bread. Damon smiled. It seemed funny to him that they were in a steak house in San Luis Obispo when they could've just as easily been back in Dallas sitting around the dinner table at home.

'What's so funny, Damon?' Larry said, rising suddenly. 'Let's get the hell out of here. I'm not hungry. I'll wait in the car.' Then, he threw his napkin down and stormed out of Angry Wade's.

Mae rose and said, 'Give me a few minutes with him.'

Damon reached out for the salt and pepper, dusting his potatoes. He swallowed them down as Mae drifted toward the door. Nothing had changed. She was still going after him, still allowing him to impose his will upon the rest of them. He despised her all of a sudden and wished he'd never agreed to come.

He thought of the day West had announced his homosexuality and how Larry had reacted.

'You suck dick?' he'd said. 'You're a . . . homo?'

Somehow, they'd gotten through it. Somehow, West and his father had come together again. Not Damon. Something irrevocable had torn inside him. When he'd told Suzanne about that day, she'd said, 'You don't have to be like him. You don't have to hate.'

But didn't he? Didn't he hate the world as much or perhaps more than Larry? He'd every right to it seemed to him. Raised by a man and woman whose only reason for staying together was because neither was capable of being alone. And love? he wondered, taking another bite of his steak. There was no love, just the congruity of

111

their respective pathologies. His father's rage, his mother's catering.

He turned to West and said, 'Tell me about Matthew.'

West's eyes were black when he turned them on Damon, who realized he'd never asked a thing about Matthew, not in all the years they'd been together.

'He's a director,' West began. 'He does porn. I write the scripts.'

'No shit,' Damon said, feeling the effects of the pot wearing off. His head felt rocky.

Damon's eyes came to rest on Mae and Larry seated in the front seat. He didn't wonder what they were saying; he already knew. 'Do you love him?' he found himself asking.

'Yes,' West said. 'I mean, it's no different from you and Suzanne or mom and dad.'

'We had nothing like them,' he said. 'We liked each other.'

West laughed which made Damon laugh as well.

He saw Suzanne stepping off the gangway in Paris, London, Tokyo. He saw her eyes fill with admiration and excitement at the thought of being someplace new. He remembered the postcards she'd sent him, still stuck to the refrigerator. Places he'd never seen. Places he'd always wanted to.

'You won't tell them about what I do,' West said. 'It's bad enough you know.'

'West, if you think for a second that I'm any less proud of you than I was a second ago, you're dumber than I thought,' Damon said.

West said, 'Suzanne said that that's what you'd say.'

Damon froze. 'When did you guys talk?' he said.

'We talked all the time, Damon,' West said. 'We used

to meet up when she had a layover in LA. She never told you?'

Damon shook his head. 'There were a lot of things we never told each other,' he said.

'The last time I saw her she said that you'd mentioned something about moving to California, by the beach,' West said. 'I'm by the beach, more or less.'

'I'll think about it,' he said, rising. 'I'm going to find out what's going on.'

'No, Damon, it's all right,' West said. 'Just drop it. I'll tell Matthew not to meet us.'

'Meet us?' Damon said. 'Who said anything about us?'

Here I am in California, Damon thought. The air, chilly and still, tingled with eucalyptus. He walked around to Larry's side of the car and tapped on the window.

'Can I talk to you for a second?' he said.

Mae wasn't crying like he thought she'd be. She sat rather loosely, playing with her face. She'd put on lipstick which made her mouth gigantic, ruined.

'Let's go,' Larry said and started the car. 'Where's your brother?'

'He's eating his dinner,' Damon said. 'We came here to eat.'

'Don't take that tone with your father,' Mae said.

Something inside him broke off.

'Get out of the car, pop,' he said.

Damon took a step backward, as Larry climbed out of the car.

'What?' he said. 'What is it, Damon?'

For a moment, Damon was looking up at his giant of a father all over again, huddled against the doorframe, while Mae looked on in wonder and silence.

113

He said, 'You want to know the real reason I was late yesterday getting to West's house?'

'Not particularly,' Larry said.

'I was arguing with a clerk,' he said. 'I called him a faggot.'

'Good for you,' Larry said.

'My brother's a faggot, pop,' he said. 'He's your son. You have a faggot for a son.'

Mae climbed out of the car and stood there, staring off into the distance.

'Your brother's condition is no concern of yours,' Larry said.

'Condition? Jesus Christ, pop. It's not a condition. It's simply what it is,' Damon said.

'Since when have you been such a philosopher?' Larry said. 'It must be all that pot you smoke. Is that it?'

In the parking lot, cars came and went, headlights cutting across their faces. For a moment, Damon finally saw what Larry's rage had done to each of them, and he shuddered.

'Pop, you're going home,' Damon said, his voice a lot like Larry's, which startled him. 'I'm putting you on a bus and sending you home.'

'Mae, did you hear what he just said to me?' Larry said but Mae wasn't there. She was nowhere in fact. 'Now look what you've done? Happy now, Damon? You've really screwed this entire trip up, you know that? Your mother was the one who begged me to invite you. She said she wouldn't go unless you came too.'

Damon thought suddenly of Suzanne and how he'd expressed to her his concerns about growing into his father.

'I'm glad Suzanne's not here to see this. It's embarrassing. You're embarrassing,' he said.

'If anyone's embarrassing, it's that brother of you.
Larry said, turning toward West who was standing a fe..
yards away, smoking. 'See that, there? He smokes to
spite me.'

Damon said, 'No, pop, he smokes because he smokes.'

'Don't give me that crap,' Larry said. 'Smoking kills.
Any smart person knows that. You don't see us
smoking. It's a low-class habit.'

West approached them and said, 'Where's mom?'

Larry was the first to call out her name. A cry rather
than a call. Larry walked in circles around the lot. West
went back into the restaurant to check the bathroom.
Damon thought he'd seen her walk toward the highway
and headed that direction.

'Do you see what I have to put up with?' Larry said.
'So don't you tell me about embarrassing when your
mother embarrasses me like this. Sometimes, in the
middle of the night, I wake up and she's gone and I pray
that she's really gone.'

Damon felt like taking his father in his arms and
squeezing until there was nothing left. He felt like
dousing his father in a bucket of ice cold water and
saying, 'Wake up, this isn't a dream. This is your life.'

A car alarm sounded and Damon moved away from
Larry. 'Where are you going?' he said.

He found Mae sitting behind the wheel of their rental
car. He had no idea how she'd gotten there. Her cheeks
were moist. She sat there, unmoving, the window down;
and Damon knew then that she'd heard everything.

Every once in a while, her streaked face was lit up by
the approach of a car into the lot. How did we get to
this place? he wondered as Larry and West appeared.

'Mom, we're heading back to the hotel,' Damon said.

Mae shook her head and climbed out of the car.

She said, 'When you and West were boys, your father and I lay in bed at night and wondered what you were going to be when you grew up. Damon, we thought for sure you'd go to law school. You were always arguing. And West, well, you were such a ham. Do you remember when you dressed up in nana's nightgown and put on that show? You made us laugh, West. We thought we'd given birth to a comedian.'

'Mae, let's go now,' Larry said, coming up beside her and taking her arm.

'You kids are our worst nightmare,' Mae said.

'Mom,' West said.

'No, West, you listen to me. And that goes for Damon as well,' she said, looking at Larry. 'He put a roof over your heads and food on the table every single day of your lives and this is the thanks he gets. This is the thanks I get?'

'Come on, Mae,' Larry said, urging her back into the car.

'I'm hungry,' she said. 'I want to eat my dinner and then I want to take some pictures and then I want to go back to the hotel and watch some TV.'

Larry and West followed her as she moved slowly up to Angry Wade's. Damon watched them take their seats at the table. He saw the waitress and the faces of the other diners. Something capsized inside of him. He thought of Suzanne again and how she wouldn't marry him.

Damon got behind the wheel of the car, the keys still in the ignition. He fumbled through his wallet for the joint and lit it. He turned on the radio and listened for a familiar song. He thought about starting the engine, about driving back to the hotel. He thought about seeking out Lilly. A plane passed effortlessly above him, a tiny red speck among the constellations. Damon shut off the radio, took a long, slow hit off the joint. He held the smoke in his lungs all the way to the door of Angry Wade's, knowing that within minutes he'd be ravenous again.

# things you can expect from your loved ones

While the crickets chirrup beyond the walls of the Blums'
bedroom, Ruth awakens, thrust out of sleep by a terrible
dream – of airplanes splitting apart in midair, shrapnel
and bloody limbs landing in her front yard. She gropes
for her pills on the nightstand. Her fingers throb, her
fifty-nine-year-old heart beats hard in her chest. The
pills, she thinks, where the hell did I put my pills? She
rummages through the drawers of the beat-up nightstand: past pictures of Daniel; piles of recipes that desperately need to be filed; the dreaded manila envelope
she hasn't dared think about, although it's been in the
same spot for over a month. I'm living in a state of
confusion, she thinks, hobbling to the bathroom. And
I'd like a one-way ticket to someplace else.

She slides the door closed and switches on the light.
Thinning, auburn hair, her father's high, intelligent
forehead, her mother's wattle. Her insomniac's blue eyes
stare back at her from the mirror, wide and glassy.
Horrified, she turns away, and there are her pills, on top
of the toilet, on top of Norman's latest issue of *Success*

magazine. She lets out a tiny O as she fiddles with the cap. And under her breath, she curses the young, ambitious do-gooders in Ohio or wherever they are – 'Damn them and their childproof lids,' she says. She composes a nasty letter in her head as she abandons the pills and climbs back into bed.

In five hours, Cliff's plane will touch down and the weekend will be set in motion. The weekend of the unveiling of Daniel's tombstone. She flexes her hands, and winces. A year ago, I opened the toughest bottles. A year ago, I went speed-walking around the neighbourhood, she thinks. She shuts her eyes against the sight of her hands, and tries not to cry.

Ruth opens her eyes as the sun dips into the room and falls across the furniture. For a moment, she has no idea where she is.

'I feel claustrophobic,' she says to Norman, already awake. 'Move the furniture back.'

'But, Ruth,' he says, drawing himself out of bed. 'You said it made the room look bigger.'

'I never said any such thing,' she says.

She seems to remember thinking at one time the room needed to be opened up. Still, knowing this doesn't account for much. She loses things somewhere between the last few seconds of day and the first seconds of sunlight.

'Are you all right?' Norman asks from the bathroom. 'Do you want me to call Dr Murphy?'

'I'm fine,' she says, slipping into her robe.

Her hands are barely moveable; her knees swollen like cantaloupe. Any other day, she might stay in bed but today this is impossible. She escapes into Daniel's room to finish tidying it up.

When Daniel went away to New York, the Blums replaced the bed with a futon, one of those metal-framed numbers with an expensive mattress cover and throw pillows. They sold the teak desk and nightstand and bought a couple of filing cabinets. Against one wall is a bookcase, full of dusty cookbooks and even dustier home-repair manuals. For a while, Norman planned on adding an extension to the house but hasn't gotten around to it. Something Ruth has had a hard time forgiving him for, since it would make living there more bearable. She hates their house, with its faux wood panelling and dark brown carpet. She's tried over the years to talk Norman into moving but he simply shrugs her off.

'When your pension kicks in,' he usually says, 'then we'll think about it.'

Ruth teaches geometry to sophomores at the local high school. And though she loves the sense of order it brings to her rather disorderly life, she can't imagine ever going back there. Since Daniel's death, the thought of standing up in front of a classroom terrifies her. She has three long summer months to decide what to do. One more box to pack up and I'm done, she thinks, running a finger along a shelf devoted to books on grieving. Elaine gave them to her, when her own daughter died of leukaemia, and said, 'These really helped me through the worst of it.'

Out in the kitchen, Norman says, 'Do you want me to come with you to the airport?'

The open pill bottle sits beside her bowl.

'No, I don't,' she says, counting out three pills. 'And while I'm gone, how about trimming the ivy away from the trees like you promised?'

Norman looks up at her, sprinkles a handful of cheddar cheese over his grits, and says, 'Yes, dear.'

A year ago. A strange man on the other end of the telephone telling her in between sobs the news about Daniel. The voice kept repeating her name, Ruth Blum, as though he weren't sure he'd dialled the right number. Everything he said ended with a question mark so that even she felt he'd made a mistake. Hadn't he?

Ruth still hasn't gotten over the way she handled the news, as if it were happening to someone else entirely. She expected to react differently, to run through the house screaming, to chop off all her hair, to set fire to the backyard. But she isn't this kind of woman. She's more like her mother than she cares to admit.

She recalls her mother's absolutely bizarre behaviour after her father died of a massive coronary. For many months, she condemned her mother's gunshot wedding. She refused to speak to her when she called; she made excuses not to visit. No wedding gift was sent, no note of kindness or congratulation.

She summed it up for Elaine: 'Fifty-seven years of marriage, escaping Hitler, building a life together in America mean nothing to her. Well, it means something to me. Where is her loyalty, I ask you?'

Almost ten years ago, the cruelty of silence was a part of her youth. She regrets those months, wishes she could have seen past the loneliness, past the arbitrariness of marrying a man half her age. When she finally spoke to her mother again, things between them were strained. She didn't recognize this other woman or what she was saying about her father and it frightened her.

'I loved your father,' her mother said, 'but I never should've married him. Frank makes me feel like a teenager. We went dancing last night, Ruth. And then we stayed up to watch the sunrise. It was the most romantic evening I've ever had.'

'You're in shock, mother,' she said. 'You don't know what you're saying.'

'If this is shock, darling, then I'm loving it,' her mother replied.

Ruth imagined that beneath the glibness, the giddiness, lurked the mother she had always known. Teutonic, cold, brutal. They spoke every Sunday and each time they did, she expected the same thing – this other woman to emerge. But she never did.

Feelings haunt her, especially the feelings of not having done enough when her mother was alive. That if she'd been a better daughter, she might have made a better mother. This same principle she applies to Daniel as well. If I'd been a better mother, she thinks, he might still be alive.

Ruth grips the steering wheel tightly in her fingers. Everyone handles grief differently, she thinks, easing the window down to grab the short-term parking ticket. She hears her heart, like rain against glass. She catches her face in the rearview mirror and gasps. When she left the house, Ruth was sure she'd put on some makeup, a little lipstick at least. Now, the face staring back at her is blank as any note she might have found among Daniel's possessions. If only he'd left a note, she thinks. There wasn't any note, not even a goodbye.

At the gate, passengers pour off the gangway, bewildered, arms loaded down with bags. She looks for Daniel among them, always looks for him in a crowd, as if the last year were nothing more than a magic trick. Sometimes, she convinces herself that it is and any day, Daniel will call and say, 'Come to New York, mom. We'll take in a show.'

All around her, sons and mothers are reunited. She

watches them in horror, seeing how easily they take this singular, beautiful moment for granted. Just like Ruth used to do. Pain is hearing the word mother in an airport on a bright and sunny summer day, she thinks.

While she looks through her purse for her lipstick, a hand touches her shoulder and she jumps.

'Ruth Blum?' the man says gingerly. She wheels around slowly and faces him. She's carried around a picture of Cliff in her mind, which barely matches the man before her. For one thing, this man is tall and thin and black. For another, he's strangely familiar-looking. She recognizes something in his eyes, set diligently into his wide face. The full lips, the angular jaw. 'Cliff Williams, pleased to meet you.'

'Oh, yes, well, we – me and my husband – we're so pleased you could make it. It means so much to us that you're here,' she says, though she never expected Cliff to come in the first place. In fact, when he'd called last month to ask if he could stay, she'd done her best to talk him out of it.

It was Norman who'd said, 'It's not like we don't have the room, Ruth. Three days go fast. You'll see.'

In the car, Ruth thinks about the last PFLAG (Parents and Friends of Lesbians and Gays) meeting she went to months ago. Many years later and she still blames herself, as any mother might, for Daniel's homosexuality. Elaine, who runs the bi-weekly meetings, told her that getting used to it was like getting used to an amputated limb. But for Ruth it's more like getting over the surprising idea that she never knew her own son. Like when she accidentally found, while cleaning up Daniel's room one afternoon, a stash of magazines: *Playgirl*, *Hustler*, *Cherry*, *Swank*, *Kandi*, *Lick*. She counted over a hundred of them scattered under his bed.

124

She didn't wonder how or where or why he'd gotten them. He was a teenager, awkward and gaunt, he spent hours in the bathroom, lighting candles and listening to Bauhaus. He wore a lot of black.

On the way home, Cliff says, 'I hope you don't mind but I took it upon myself to invite the cast of *Lions and Tigers and Bears, Oh My.*'

This was Daniel's last Broadway show, an all-male revue, in which he played The Great and Powerful Oz. The show was a tell-all, told from the point of view of the Wicked Witch of the West. Cliff played the Wicked Witch.

'No, not at all,' Ruth says, though she can't imagine what sort of people might show up.

'Daniel was quite an Oz,' Cliff says. 'A wonderful wizard.'

'Yes, we read a review of the show,' she says. 'I wish we could've seen it.'

'Luckily, we're starting the roadshow in about a month,' Cliff says. 'I'll get you tickets.'

'Splendid,' Ruth says. 'I've always thought the witch got the short end of the stick. It's about time someone shone a little light on her suffering, too.'

Cliff says, 'Well, I'm glad you see it that way. A lot of folks think that what we're doing sort of goes against everything L. Frank Baum stood for. The guy was a communist, did you know that?'

'No, I did not,' Ruth says as she pulls into the parking lot of Winston Churchill High School. Mid afternoon and the sun is beginning its slow descent. Ruth smells Cliff beside her, his aftershave, which Daniel might have given him. She wrings her hands.

'I have to run inside quickly,' she says, 'to pick up a box of stuff. I'll only be a minute.'

'I'll wait here, I guess,' Cliff says, lighting a cigarette while rolling down his window.

Ruth wanders into the building, startled by its disquietude. Men wax the floors as other men paint the lockers. One black, one red; the school colours. Someone's screwed up this arrangement: three black lockers in a row. She wants to point out this snafu but doesn't. She isn't there to instruct; she's there to get her box and go home. But she can't help lingering in the hall. Something undeniably lovely about being in school when school isn't going on around her. Almost beautiful, this afternoon before the halls fill up for the summer.

(After explaining to her boss, Principal Burkehardt, that she needed the summer off, she broke down and told him about Norman and Elaine. She hadn't meant to say anything; it just slipped out. Principal Burkehardt told her to take as much time as she needed; he said he understood, since his own wife had left him for a mechanic.)

Ruth looks out her classroom window. In the parking lot, she notices the grit and grime on the roof of her car and a message etched into the dust of the rear windshield: *I love you!*

She gathers up the box. Files, folders, her 'Teacher of the Year' award, rulers, graph paper, protractors, all the things that mean so much less now that they are crammed in a box. Before she leaves, Ruth goes to the bathroom at the end of the hall, and catches sight of Cliff strolling toward the football field. She applies some lipstick, and, box in arms, hurries to the car.

The trunk overflows with junk: some of Norman's old shirts she's been meaning to give to Goodwill, an unusable spare tyre, a stack of newspapers, a box of

Daniel's full of what she doesn't recollect. She places her box in the backseat and then pulls this smaller box out. Using one of Norman's shirts, she smears *I love you!* off the rear windshield and heads toward the bleachers.

Cliff sits on the risers, smoking a cigarette. He waves at her from across the field, a curl of smoke escaping out his mouth.

He calls, 'Are you ready to go?'

'Not quite,' she says, rearranging the box in her arms.

Far heavier than she anticipated, she wonders what part of Daniel's life hides inside it. She wants to open it but is afraid of what she may find. More magazines, hateful letters to her he never sent? Some things are better left unknown.

She's not too sure how Cliff will react when he sees what she is about to do. If he wants an explanation, she thinks, I'll simply say that compulsivity often accompanies grief.

In the centre of the overgrown field, she lowers the box down. She extracts the lighter fluid and matches from her purse. For a moment, she realizes how crazy this must seem but she doesn't care; grief is crazy.

'Mrs Blum, are you all right?' he says.

'Don't tell Norman,' she says, as the wind blows out match after match. 'I read about this in a book.'

Cliff takes another drag of his cigarette.

'Isn't this against the law?' he says. 'I mean, public fires.'

'This is Texas,' she says. 'Everything's against the law.'

This isn't the first time Ruth's set fire to a box of Daniel's things. The first week after his suicide, she packed up a box of his books and burned it in Goodwill's parking lot.

'I don't know what this means to you,' he says, 'but I guess it's really important.'

'Yes, it is,' she says. She opens her hand and Cliff places his lighter in it. 'Thank you.'

Ruth, thumb poised on the lighter, looks around her. No one, nothing.

The box catches instantly.

The sun hangs low in the sky, shadowing the field and the school. Soon, the fireflies and June bugs will come out and the air will fill with a different kind of light. Ruth looks forward to this light as things lose their angles and softly fade. When she can look at Norman and feel something stir, something besides regret.

In a matter of minutes, the box is a smouldering pile. Ruth stamps out the last of the remaining embers and then the two head back to the car.

At the house, Ruth shows Cliff to Daniel's room and says, 'If you need anything, I'll be in the kitchen. There are towels in the bathroom. The knobs are funny. You have to play with them. Norman should be home soon. We like to eat at six sharp.'

Cliff stands with his back to her, his face folded in shadows. From this angle, he seems much smaller to her; his suit hangs off him like a drape. But maybe this is simply an illusion. Men carry their grief differently, she read, shrinking into it rather than expanding away from it. While a woman's grief is lodged inside her body, a man's is a reflection of posture, his clothing. She senses this about Cliff as she closes the door behind her.

Halfway down the hall, she hears Elaine and Norman.

'Ruth,' Norman calls, 'are you home?'

She stops short of the doorway. Behind her, sunlight falls from the window, catching the multitude of stains in the brown shag carpet. An urge comes over her to get on her hands and knees with a sponge; instead, she'll call a cleaning service later. And yet every time she goes to the Yellow Pages, she has trouble remembering why. As if between thought and action, she has slipped into another universe. She can't explain it.

'Here I am,' she says, smiling, 'What's all the fuss about, Norman? Oh, hello, Elaine.'

Norman rises and greets her warmly with a kiss on the cheek. Ruth watches Elaine watching them and a momentary scowl slips nearly unnoticed across Elaine's tanned face. She's a handsome woman, with frosted blond hair and large cat eyes. Always smelling of expensive perfumes, Elaine works at a department store, selling speciality soaps.

'We ran into each other in the mall,' Norman says, holding a bouquet of flowers out for her. 'Where's Cliff?'

Ruth says, 'I think he's taking a nap. Did you know, dear, that Cliff is an actor on Broadway?'

'I just think it's *marvellous* that you invited him this weekend,' Elaine says perkily. 'It really shows how *far* you've come.'

'Yes, well, I don't know about how far we've come,' Ruth says, going into the kitchen. 'But I do know how far I'd like to go.'

To Elaine, Norman says uncomfortably, 'Let me walk you to your car.'

'Yes,' Elaine says, rising, though it is Ruth who takes her by the arm. 'We really did run into each other at the mall, Ruth.'

Ruth says, squeezing Elaine's arm until she feels bone, 'I'll have those books back to you next week,' and sort of half-hurls Elaine out the front door.

I'll leave her a little present in her front yard, Ruth thinks.

Norman puts on the TV. Ruth takes a seat at the opposite end of the couch. The flowers sit in a vase on the kitchen table, already wilted. Even from where she sits, she feels the heat of Norman's body. It makes her aware of how cold she's been the entire day. Suddenly, she wants to kiss him, the way they used to when Daniel was asleep and they had the house to themselves.

Norman says, 'I have to check on the stocks,' and leaves her to the TV. She follows him into his study, a place usually off-limits to her. The chime of the computer and she knows she's lost him again. He will sit for hours, charting his portfolios and retirement funds.

'Are you planning on mowing the yard?' she asks.

'Yes,' he says. 'Are you planning on using that tone of voice with me for the rest of our lives?'

'What tone is that?'

'Ruth, one day we're going to have to talk about –'

'No,' she says. 'No, we don't have to talk about anything, Norman. I just want to get through the next couple of days.'

'Okay,' he says. 'But you can't tell me that I haven't tried.'

She watches the screen come to life with flashing boxes and dollar signs. She rests her hands on Norman's chair. She almost kisses the back of his neck.

After dinner, Norman and Cliff sit outside on the patio, discussing the stock market. It seems that Norman has found an ally and this helps her relax. Though she finds this hobby of his – gambling with their life savings – somewhat horrifying. She remembers that day in 1987, Black Tuesday, when their IBM stock fell fifty-six points and they lost half a million dollars. They took a second mortgage out on the house. The money was not the issue – not to Ruth anyway. The issue was funding Daniel's college education.

She remembers the afternoon he came home from high school after track practice. She was finishing up dinner and as he came through the door, she said, 'Danny, we have to have a talk.'

She wanted to bear his anger and disappointment because she was his mother, because they were closer.

'We can't afford Cornell,' she said. 'You're going to have to make other arrangements.'

'What are you talking about, mom?' he said.

'We were a bit reckless,' she said.

'I understand,' he said.

She was surprised by his reaction, more grown-up than she had thought he'd be, more resigned than she had hoped for.

'If it's important to you, I'm sure you'll find a way,' she said offhandedly.

On the wall of his bedroom, she looks for the missing diploma, the graduation pictures never taken. She hates herself for not being the kind of woman strong enough to handle her husband. Daniel might still be alive, she thinks, if you'd been a different kind of woman.

She shuts the door, lies on the futon face-first, and screams into the pillow. She screams and screams, pushing her voice down into every fibre of the pillow, the mattress, the carpet beneath. She screams for five minutes straight without stopping, just one long continuous scream that burns her throat, shakes her teeth.

When she is done, she gets up, straightens the futon, and then, suddenly, she goes to the closet. Her joints ache as she reaches up and takes down a box marked TAXES, 1985. She pulls the dusty, cardboard lid off and peers down at Daniel's bright and glossy magazines.

She sees what Daniel must have: the candy-eyed girls with large lips, the men with smooth unadulterated skin. She comes to *Playgirl*. On the cover, a man who resembles Cliff. Ten years younger, the exposé speaks of Cliff's likes and dislikes when it comes to women. He likes a girl who reads Shakespeare; he dislikes a girl without a sense of humour. The pictures of Cliff reveal ridges of muscle and a navel ring. Ruth runs a crooked finger over Cliff's face and thinks, The world is a strange place and I'm a stranger in it. My best friend sleeps with my husband and my child jumps off a forty-storey building.

She lugs the box into the den and, on one of the shelves above the *Encyclopaedia Britannica*, Ruth locates the bowl of matches. She's never understood why Norman collects matches since neither of them smoke, since they have no fireplace. People collect all sorts of stupid things, she thinks, passing the bay window.

The moon through the trees lights up the men's faces. Norman sits in his discussion posture, feet extended in front of him, one curled over the other. Cliff raises a hand across his face to bat away a mosquito. They discuss. Their faces are serious, potent. Ruth tries to read Norman's lips and, catching random words – sick, marriage, wife – decides that she can't despise him for his affair with Elaine any more than she can despise herself for allowing it to happen.

She walks past Norman and Cliff with the box and out into the yard.

Norman says, 'Ruth, Jesus, not again.'

This is the sixth box in a year.

'Why don't you just set the whole house on fire?' Norman says.

'Why don't I just set you on fire,' she replies.

Cliff stares up into the trees, shifting uncomfortably. He lights a cigarette. Ruth sets the box down on the spot where the pecan tree used to be.

'Think about the neighbours,' Norman calls. 'They aren't going to like this.'

'So who cares. We don't like our neighbours, Norman,' she calls back. 'Besides, this is half of my property.'

'Thirty-seven years of marriage and this is what I have to show for it,' she says to the box. 'Half an acre of land, a husband who cheats on me, a house I hate, a dead son, and the Wicked Witch of the West on my patio.'

The box catches on her first try.

She turns to face Norman, who now wields the garden hose.

'Step away from the box,' he says.

'You bastard,' she says.

'Get away from the box, Ruth,' he says. 'Don't make me do it.'

Ruth digs her bare feet into the soft, cool grass. 'Blast away,' she says.

A stream of water hits her in the face. Behind her, the box burns steadily; she feels its heat on her neck and arms.

'You'll have to do better than that, old man,' she says.

Cigarette in hand, Cliff makes his way between the Blums. He closes his eyes and draws a hand across his face, which becomes, when his hand lowers, the face of the Wicked Witch of the West. As he draws on his cigarette, Cliff sings, 'Those ruby red slippers/they hold me in their thrall/I am nothing without them/no, nothing at all'.

His counter-tenor's voice rises as he runs his hands over a pretend crystal ball. He scrunches up one shoulder. Norman increases the water pressure.

'Listen, Cliff, no offence but I'm kind of having a fight with my wife,' he says. Then, to Ruth, 'This isn't funny anymore. What if one of those sparks ignites the fence? Who's going to pay? Who?'

Cliff stops singing and turns to Ruth. 'Mrs Blum, he's right you know. This is sort of dangerous. The wind and all. Who knows what could happen?'

In the distance, the sound of sirens as Ruth thinks about the manila envelope in her drawer, the pictures of Elaine and Norman.

When Norman accidentally hits Cliff with the water, Ruth says, 'Norman, you idiot.'

Cliff raises a hand up to his face again, either to wipe away the water or prevent another attack.

'Not a problem,' he says and disappears into the house.

Norman sprays Ruth until she can no longer tell the difference between the water on her face and her own tears. She turns to the box, and he shoots her back. The fire warms her, the smoke curling into the air. The ink in the magazines colours the flames blue and green and pink.

'This is no way for a grown woman to act,' Norman shouts.

'I could say the same for a friend of yours,' Ruth shouts back.

Norman finally turns off the hose, says, 'I'm calling the fire department,' and leaves.

Ruth, slightly chilly, stands above the box and waits until the last embers die.

*

That night, her arthritis unbearable, Ruth climbs out of
bed and instead of the pills, she pours herself a jigger of
brandy. It's the same bottle they've had on the shelf at
the back of the cupboard for years. The same one they
shared the first night they spent in the house. She drinks
it down and then refills it. Drinks this down, too. She
stares out the bay window at the ivy snaking its way up
into the trees. She's angry and tired and her body hurts
as if God himself has taken a mallet to it.

After a while, Ruth doesn't feel angry or tired or hurt.
She's drunk. For the first time in years. She goes into
the living room, where Norman's hi-fi, a relic from
the 1970s, sits against the wall. Ruth rifles through the
albums. She puts on *Pink Moon* and sings along. She
drinks straight from the bottle of brandy. She thinks
nothing of Daniel or Norman or Cliff, nothing of the
cemetery, the mourners, the prayer for the dead. Nick
Drake croons and she loves him. The rich warmth of his
voice, the smooth texture in her ears. She drinks. And
dances.

She imagines the parties never thrown and the wine
never spilled. The trips never taken and the houses never
built. She dreams of another boy, the real love of her
life, Steven Melman. And dances with him around the
room until the album ends and she is dizzy and giddy
and sad. She drops the bottle to the carpet.

Before going back to bed, she stops at Cliff's door.
She presses an ear up against it. The house shifts under
her – the foundation, the floor, everything unsettling.
She loses her balance, plants a hand on the wall. Her
throat burns. She burps. In her haze, the phone rings and
it is Daniel thanking her for showing him how to be The
Great and Powerful Oz.

Opening the door, she wobbles into the room. His

135

damp face cut by moonlight, Cliff mumbles something incoherent. Lines from the play. Lines from his life. She remembers his voice over the phone last year, three thousand miles away. She remembers him saying, 'I would've called sooner but Daniel told me his parents were dead.'

Ruth thinks about jumping, as she moves silently to the bed. She leans over Cliff. She says his name. She says it again. She bends even closer to him. He opens his eyes and stares at her, surprised to find her there. Ruth reaches out and touches his face, her bony fingers painful.

She says, 'I couldn't wait to get away from my horrible mother and Daniel couldn't wait to get away from me.' She pauses. 'I don't know what happened here, in this house. I can't explain it.' She sits down on the edge of the bed.

'Mrs Blum, you should get some sleep,' Cliff says.

'I loved a boy once. It was devastating.' As soon as she says it, she feels funny, a tingling. 'I was still getting over Steven when I met Norman in the elevator of the Time-Life Building. He lavished me with expensive dinners and chocolates and flowers. Unnecessary things. And he did something no one had ever been able to do,' she says. 'He used to finish my sentences.'

Cliff says, 'You have any more scotch?'

Ruth shakes her head. 'There's some wine for tomorrow.' The clock by the bed registers four-thirty. 'Oh, my. It's . . . very late.'

'I'm usually up at this time,' Cliff says. 'I go for a run in Central Park, before all the annoying people get there.' He puts on a pair of sweatpants over his boxers and laces up his Nikes. 'I'm going for a jog.'

'If you wait, I'll drive you up to the school,' she says.

'No, that's all right,' he says. 'But if I'm not back in an hour, send out a search party.'

There is a moment, just before he disappears, that she wants to ask him: why did Daniel jump? And yet she feels that anything he says won't be enough. There aren't any words to make sense of what she's going through. This bewildering, which shifts furniture around in the middle of the night, makes people feel things that probably aren't even there.

Cliff opens the front door and wanders outside. She can almost hear him in the grass. She steps into their bedroom, closes the door, clicks on the light.

'Jesus, Ruth, what is it?' Norman says, rising up onto his elbows and rubbing his eyes. 'Do you need your pills?'

'You blame me for Daniel's death,' she says.

'Don't be absurd,' Norman says. 'It wasn't your fault.'

'I blame you,' she says. 'Someone's got to take some responsibility, Norman. I can't do it any more.'

Ruth opens a drawer in her nightstand and pulls out the manila envelope. She dumps the contents out on the bed and spreads the photos across the sheets. Pictures of Norman and Elaine, pictures she's gone over a thousand times. When the man who took the photographs delivered them to her, he said, 'Prepare yourself.'

Norman reaches out to touch her and she withdraws.

'Ruth, please,' he says. 'This isn't what it looks like.'

'Don't patronize me,' she says and flexes her burning fingers. She reaches down for one picture in particular. Norman and Elaine lying on a grassy lawn with the University of Texas's Main Building in the background. The Spanish tiled roof glimmers in the sunlight, and all around them hangs the spiny fruit of Mesquite trees.

'The three of us used to go there all the time,' she says. 'God, I feel like an idiot.'

'Oh, Jesus,' Norman says. 'Listen to me –'

'I've been listening to you for years,' she says and gathers the photos in her hands. 'We've never been happy together.'

She replaces the photos in the envelope, dresses, and then walks out the door.

Envelope in hand, Ruth moves slowly through the field to the bleachers. She marvels at how everything is exactly as it was when Daniel used to run here. She remembers coming to watch him jump the hurdles, the way he flew from one to the other. His speed was uncanny and she wondered where he'd gotten it.

She pulls out a picture of Norman, his face full of an expression – happiness, relief, joy – she hasn't seen in ages. The same expression when she told him he was going to be a father. Having a baby was supposed to hold us together, she thinks, taking out the matches. But then, with bloated fingers, she begins to fold the picture, first one corner then another. There is something in the folding, turning something flat and square into an object of dimension and depth. And she realizes that this is what loss really is: sharp corners, hard edges, unknowable quantities. For a moment, she cradles this odd arrangement of paper in her hands. Then, she stands up and sails it into the air, where it catches briefly, soaring.

# most of us are here against our will

The banner – *Let's Give Our Children a Safe Place to Play* – hangs between two telephone poles in the parking lot of General Omar Bradley High School. I didn't go to school here. I didn't grow up in Galveston, where we are. I'm from someplace else.

Tonight, as usual, we sit in a circle in the physics classroom, our chairs almost touching. This is the tenth week in a twelve-week instructional on *How to Write Your Way Out of Hysteria*. It seems that we've all signed up for these meetings because someone in our family decided we were a threat to ourselves. Bob's my only family. There is also Camilla Rae, my best friend, but she is out of her mind right now. There's no Camilla Rae without hysteria.

I check my watch. We've been here almost three-quarters of an hour. In another few minutes, Dr Saunders will announce our break. Class runs two hours, give or take. There are eight people – five men, three women. The men sit drawn-up and hunched, in league with one another; the women eye them suspiciously. Sometimes, I eye them suspiciously too. I'm not sure why. I'm not sure why I do half the things I do. That's partly why I'm here.

When Dr Saunders announces our ten-minute break, I head directly outside to smoke. I stand there, looking up at our classroom window. There is the silhouette of Camilla (not Camilla Rae) – she looks more like a Carol or a Harriet – eating one of the tuna fish sandwiches. I never eat what Dr Saunders brings in. I am never hungry this time of night. Not for food anyway.

Back inside, Dr Saunders reads a selection from his latest, bestselling book, *Writing Your Way Out of Hysteria*. 'Love may lead us all to a door of unlimited and wonderful possibility,' he chants, 'but it is only through a love of language – the very backbone of life on this planet – that we can unlock these great doors to get at Peace. Words too can lead us to the same door. This takes practice. Each word is a universe, a destiny. In the beginning was the Word and the Word was God. It is up to us, then, to choose them very carefully. Do not waste words, for only they have the power to change you.' When he is done, he looks at us thoughtfully. 'I believe that tonight Camilla will read to us.'

This is his plan: to get us to open ourselves up through words. Logotherapy, he calls it.

Camilla rises and goes to the podium at the head of the room. She won't meet anyone's eyes. Her voice barely makes it out to me. I strain to listen to this forty-six-year-old woman and mother of three tell us about being raped in the Sears & Roebuck's parking lot.

When she ends, she stands there not knowing what to do. Tears leak down her face. The room is deadly still as Dr Saunders says, 'Camilla, is there anything you would like to do to the man who did this?'

She says hesitantly, 'I, I don't know what to say. I'm not sure.'

'You're safe here, Camilla. Say anything you want to. We're here to help you,' Dr Saunders says gently, looking around the room at us.

I don't know what to say either. What can you say to someone who isn't there? Camilla tries. She closes her eyes. She grips the edges of her desk, which is too small for her. Her knuckles go white. She says, through gritted teeth, while looking straight at Dr Saunders, 'I want you to know what it feels like not to be able to look anyone in the eye. I want to bash your goddamn head in. I want to ruin your life.' She pauses. Then, 'Why did you do this to me? I never did anything to you.' There are no tears.

'There's no reason anyone will be able to give you to explain why he did what he did,' Dr Saunders says. 'You're angry, Camilla. It's all right to be angry.'

'The police say it's probably someone I knew. Isn't that ridiculous? I don't know anyone who would do anything like that.' Her voice is a wilderness and sounds like my mother's.

Glen, a wispy man in his early thirties, raises his hand and says, 'You are so courageous! I know exactly what you mean. When it happened to me, I thought the same thing.' Glen and his brother slept in the same bed for years. Glen says that his brother attacked him but I'm not sure I believe him. Every story is similar, including my own. It's hard to believe anyone. 'I despise men,' he adds. 'Every one of you is sick.'

'Now, Glen,' Dr Saunders says. 'We cannot go around making accusations like that. You cannot sentence every man the same.'

The man on my left, Kenny, having something to say about everything, says, smirking, 'He probably deserved it. You were probably the kind of kid that tortured animals, weren't you?'

'Fuck you, Kenny,' Glen says. 'There's only one person I'd like to torture right now.' He makes scissors out of two fingers and slices the air. 'That should make the world a safer place.'

'Kenny, Glen, enough,' Dr Saunders says. 'I understand both of you are here for very different reasons and that is the point of this workshop. Bringing you together to work all of this out.' He looks at the clock. 'Unfortunately, I'm afraid we've run out of time.'

Kenny and Glen aren't their real names. Marvin isn't my name either. We aren't allowed to use our real names in class. (I call it class; no one else does.) Dr Saunders passed out a list of names that first evening.

As far as I could remember, Marvin was the only one that wasn't the name of a hurricane.

Outside, I pull out a Pall Mall and set my lips on the foam-rubber filter. I always wet the end first, a trick I learned years ago from Steven. He said it made the smoke taste better. I read in a magazine, though, that it could reduce my risk of cancer.

Walking slowly, I wonder if Bob is waiting for me. I don't want to go home just yet. The wind picks up newspapers, coffee lids, candy wrappers, swirling them around at my feet. I crunch a half-full can of Fresca under my foot, then pick it up and drop-kick it. My hands are sticky and smell like grapefruit. Another silly reminder of my stepfather.

When I get home, Bob is watching TV. He says, 'Camilla Rae just called. She said you were having dinner with her tonight? I thought we were going bowling, Glen. I told her to fuck herself.' Bob smiles. I admire his honesty. He is the only person I know who doesn't put up with Camilla Rae. Who sees through all her hippie ways. Who thinks she is trying to break us up, which may or may not be true.

'You're not at work,' I say, sitting down beside him. 'I thought you'd be working tonight.'

'I took it off – remember? – so that we could spend some time together,' he says, playing with the remote.

A car pulls up outside and honks. We both look at the window. Camilla Rae sits in our crushed oyster-shell, crescent-shaped driveway, smoking. She will not come inside.

'Why do I always have to be the bad guy?' I say. I have known Camilla Rae as long as I've known Bob. Longer than Bob actually since we didn't get together until later.

'Hey, what do you call a person that comes into your life and messes it all up?' This is a joke that Bob has made up. The answer sits on my lips as I head toward the door. 'You call a person that comes into you life and messes it all up – you call him Glen. That's what you call him.'

'And what do you call a person who signed Glen up for a class he didn't want to take?' I say, stepping out the door.

Bob stands at the window and then the lights go off. Soon, he will put on his bowling shirt and sit in the dark, calling out his answers to the TV.

In the car, Camilla Rae says, 'You look like a man without a name, a dog without a bone.' It's a line from a song, a song we used to sing on the way to the beach.

'It's a whole lot worse than that,' I say.

'I have just the thing for that,' she says and points to a sign for 99-cent margaritas at Taco Cabana.

After we've ordered some nachos and sit down, Camilla Rae locates the locket around her neck and opens it. The contents – a few oddly shaped pills – roll onto the table. I don't ask her what they are. I stopped asking a long time ago.

('Echinacea and valerian root,' she always says, winking. 'You should take them.')

'So this thing happened with Brad and now I'm totally confused,' she says, dropping a pill onto her tongue. 'But what makes it all so much worse is . . .' As I wait for her to continue, our eyes stray to the couple beside us at the next table. Their children lob bits of *pico de gallo* over the railing. 'I have a little Brad growing inside me,' she whispers.

Our number is called and she goes to the counter. Long tan legs, freshly shaven, the dress I bought her dotted with tiny sunflowers, overexposed skin, the stained macramé anklet from some flea market. She pulls at the skin under her chin, one hand bent at her narrow waist. She is indeed the daughter of flower children. Though Camilla Rae is more than that. She is Dylan's love child, a rolling stone. Through the window, I look at the Gulf of Mexico. The sky is darkening, the Galveston air heavy and laced with salt.

'I'm sorry about Bob,' I say, tasting the margarita.

'That's all right. I'm used to him by now. I just never thought you'd stay with a woman-hater.'

'Bob's not a woman-hater,' I say. 'He's just a little protective.'

'What does that mean?' she says.

'Bob worries that you're trying to take me away,' I say.

'How could I do that? You like boys,' Camilla Rae says. 'That's pretty stupid of him.'

'You know how guys are. Either you're theirs

completely or not at all. No middle ground. It's getting harder and harder to be with him, though,' I say.

'Why? Has he hit you again?' she says.

'No, nothing like that,' I say.

Bob is not the gentlest man I've ever been with. But he is good to me. He holds me when it's necessary. I laugh a lot at the way he is, blustery and hard but often childish and silly. He has just about everything I want: a house, a car, the strength to keep me when I'd just as soon walk away. Sometimes, though, I get the feeling I deserve better than Bob.

'Well, good, because if he ever lays another finger on you,' she says, 'I'm going to send Brad over there to show him what it feels like.'

'Thanks for the support,' I say.

'We need each other,' she says, licking the salt around the rim of the glass. 'I don't think I can have this baby without you.'

'That is terrible,' Bob says the next morning. It seems he has completely forgotten about last night. (Someday, though, he will bring it up again – 'Remember the time you broke our date to go with that bitch,' he will say. 'That's the problem with you, Glen. You need to recognize your enemies.')

He's standing at the door to the bathroom, water dripping off his body. The lines of his stomach tighten. The powdery scent of baby oil fills the room. Bob steps back into the bathroom. Where he has stood, he leaves the outline of a few toes, two heels. My back is to him on the bed. I am sorting our socks.

'She's a sweet woman. I just can't believe something like that happened to her,' I say. 'And in the Sears' parking lot of all places.'

'Where was Brad when all this was happening?' he says, confused.

'What in the hell are you talking about?' I say.

I study Bob's face; he is indeed confused. We have been talking about class, about Camilla. Though I've explained to him that we can't use our given names, though I've told him the other Camilla is probably a Carol or Harriet, he just won't listen. To Bob, each name should bear its own meaning.

'It was your idea for me to go to that stupid class,' I say, curtly. 'The least you can do is keep up.'

'Well, anyway,' Bob says, turning out the bathroom light. 'It's a horrible story. Just as horrible as what happened with you and Steven.'

'This isn't a contest,' I say. 'No one gets a prize for telling the worst story.'

The last time he mentioned Steven I nearly bit off my tongue. Just another reason Bob enrolled me for Dr Saunders' class. There were so many reasons by that point. Sometimes, when Bob looks at me, I think he must know the whole story. But he doesn't. I'm afraid he'll leave me when he does.

'I really don't want to talk about him,' I say. I stop what I am doing and turn toward Bob. With his hands firmly at his sides, the yellow towel carefully tucked in the crux of his hips, he raises his eyebrows; he knows there's more to it. More that I am not telling him. 'Why the sudden interest?'

He comes into the room, the sun catching the oil and water on his body.

'You woke me up last night. Again. You kept calling out his name. It doesn't look good, Glen. I think I'm a pretty patient guy, at least when it comes to you. But some things are beyond even my patience. Some things require faith, which you know I don't have.'

I want to go back to the socks – red-red, blue-blue, yellow-yellow – the still-burning, just-out-of-the-dryer smell, but I know that Bob wants more than an answer, he wants a confession.

'Steven's just this guy,' I say. 'Before I met you. He's not important. Not anymore.'

'Come on. We've been through this before,' he says. 'Don't lie to me.'

'I am not fucking around,' I say. 'I told you I didn't feel like talking about this right now, okay?'

'You never want to talk about it,' he says.

Bob takes one step backwards, then two, three, four until finally he is out the door. Seconds later the TV comes on. A woman's voice blasts the news all over the house. It is much too loud for this early in the morning, for any hour really. But this is Bob's way of settling this thing between us. And this – folding socks – is mine.

Tonight, Camilla Rae has decided that it's high time we were children again. 'And what do children do?' she asks me on the way to Westwood Park pool.

It is late, around 10:45 p.m. Brad is playing guitar as we sneak away. Bob is doing what Bob does: working. He plans to buy a new car by the end of the month. Before I moved in with him, Camilla Rae and I were always sneaking away. To the movies, to Magnolia Café for blueberry pancakes, to Taco Cabana for margaritas. Now, we are trespassing. Just another crazy night.

Even before she lands on her feet on the other side of the fence, she is already pulling off the same skimpy sundress. She cannot wait to be naked.

'Your turn,' Camilla Rae says, jumping headfirst into the pool.

Her thighs are smooth, like the spare parts of mannequins. I scale the fence. My boots land in a puddle with a squish. They are new; they are ostrich. A present from Bob. Really a bribe to get me to go to class. I told him about the boots and they appeared one day in my closet. He said the boots were his way of stamping out Steven. I thought that was nice of him, the nicest thing he'd ever said.

Once naked, there is no turning back. I take a deep breath and hurl myself into the icy water. We swim up and down the length of the pool, doggie-paddling, passing each other and spitting. My lungs fight me; they want a cigarette. I pull myself out and light two, handing one to Camilla Rae, who takes it from me willingly. 'You were reading my mind,' she says.

As I smoke, I sit on the steps, deciding which part of my body I hate the most – my skinny, underdeveloped arms or my caved-in chest. I decide on neither, since I hate all parts of my body with equal disgust. I finish the cigarette and then dive under the water. The chlorine is strong; it eats my eyes.

Camilla Rae rolls into a somersault, a backflip. Her ribs are steak knives; I can see each bone through her skin. I look down at my own ribs. A thin layer of fat hides them but since I've stopped being hungry, I can almost see them. This makes me happier than I've been in years. To see my ribs, I think. Now that would be something great.

'My mom and I used to go to Lake Michigan when I was a girl. We'd go early in the morning before anyone was there so that we could swim naked. I loved my mother's body. She was the same age I am now except my body's falling apart,' she says, 'and I'm only twenty-five. I haven't dropped acid in years. Not like her. She used to party every day while she was in grad school.'

'What do you mean "only twenty-five"?' I ask. 'It's amazing we've made it this far.'

'It's different for us.' By us, I suppose she means women. 'Our bodies talk to us every day.'

I want to ask her what hers says. As if on cue she frowns and says, 'Mine says to get married. To have children. To fulfil my duties as a mother, daughter, and a woman.'

'So deep,' I say.

She bobs up and down, her feet not touching the bottom.

'These aren't just for sucking.' She cups her boobs, bounces them on her chest. 'They're my life.'

She tweaks a nipple. 'You know I've never been much of a breast man,' I admit. 'But yours still look pretty firm – for an old woman.' Which makes me think of the other Camilla.

'Glen, you wouldn't be so mean to me if you knew what I had to carry around in this body of mine. Yeast, chlamydia, genital warts. My ob/gyn told me no sex for six weeks. Every time Brad sticks his dick in me I get a bladder infection.'

I do a headstand so that my legs shoot straight out of the water. The air is chilly above me but the water is warm. This phenomenon has always amazed me: how quickly our bodies adapt to initially painful surroundings.

'My gramma, Mimi, got married when she was eighteen. And my mother was married at twenty,' she says. 'I'm not too sure I don't want to get married next week.' She rubs her tummy. 'I've got to think about –'

'So you're having the kid?' I ask and climb out to the

edge of the high diving board. From here, the water looks like tar. Something else that could drag us down. I half expect to find the bones of lost lovers there on the floor.

'I didn't say that,' Camilla Rae calls.

I take a running leap and throw myself into the air. I hit the water hard and sink to the leafy bottom. Down there, under the water, leaving Bob doesn't seem like such a bad thing. I'll take the boots with me, though. When I resurface, Camilla Rae leans against the fence at the far end of the pool, smoking a joint. She is dressed again, wearing the boots.

'These are cool,' she says, clomping around. 'I want to get a pair for Brad. Were they expensive?'

'I can go to Sears and have a look around.'

I think about Sears: the cold asphalt of the parking lot. What words went through her head? And if he knew her, did he say her name?

'I think I'll surprise him for his birthday,' Camilla Rae says. 'Though he really doesn't deserve it.'

'Do they ever?' I say.

She grins at me. 'Yes,' she says. 'Sometimes they do.'

I followed Camilla Rae up the rickety wooden steps to her apartment. We'd met a couple weeks before at a rave. It was very late. She told me that she took the apartment because of the deck, which she used year-round. Before we went inside, we sat outside. Camilla Rae lit candles and we smoked a joint. Joni Mitchell growled through the apartment. The mosquitoes bit me through my shirt. After a while, Camilla Rae led me into the bathroom, where she laid a towel out for me. She burned jasmine incense and talked about her mother, who was living in Houston with her third husband. The knobs are backwards, she said. Cold is hot and hot is cold. While the shower ran, images of Bob came to me. Driving in his truck along the highway. Kissing him on the seawall. Leaving him there. I didn't think I'd ever see him again, which was just as well. Why go through that again? I'm going to bed, Camilla Rae shouted through the door. The couch is all set up for you. Half an hour later, I was almost asleep when the screendoor creaked open and a half-dressed boy walked inside. He wore a Metallica T-shirt and a pair of worn-out army fatigues. A bandanna hung lazily around his neck. His boots struck the floor loudly as he slipped by me on his way to Camilla Rae's bedroom. I rose on my elbows. Hey, I said. Camilla Rae in there? he said. Yeah, I said. He was drunk, that much was obvious. Who are you? he said. I'm Glen, I said. Not your name, arsehole. What're you doing here? That's when Camilla Rae came out. She stood in front of us, her robe open at the throat. Hey, she said. Get out of here. Aw, come on, baby, he said, manufacturing softness. No, I mean it, she said. You can't keep coming by here every time you want to – he slapped her, hard across the mouth so that her robe opened. I was at him then, behind him, holding him back. Fuck y'all, he screamed. I held him as tightly as I could, while Camilla Rae called one of his friends. I'm fine, he kept saying. Fine, fine, fine. Later, Camilla Rae confessed that he wasn't fine. That she'd broken up with him weeks ago but somehow he just didn't get it. He's a really nice guy when he wants to be, she said. But I knew guys like him. They weren't nice. None of them. They told you what you wanted to hear. They professed their love and anger and sorrow with fists. Each storm has a name, my mother used to tell me. That night, the storm's name was Brad.

\*

The rain starts in the morning and continues all day. Since I've been promoted to assistant manager at The Copy Desk and taken off the night shift, I've enjoyed being able to see the day. The early shift – from six a.m. to three p.m. – flies by. I feel somehow that I have more in common with the world now. I get up before Bob, who doesn't leave the bed until he has to, which is somewhere around noon. I don't mind. But there's something to be said for the hours before the city rises and things get away from you.

Through the windows, the sky is one lonesome streak of gray. I can hear the rain above me. Through the drop-ceiling, against the roof. Business is slow. The thunder and lightning keep most people indoors. Not Camilla Rae. She stops by around one with a huge brown bag from McDonald's. She lays it on the table between us and starts lifting out Big Macs, strawberry milkshakes, fries. I'm not hungry, though I take a hamburger any-way. All this while Camilla Rae tells me that Brad still doesn't know. That there hasn't been a right moment to tell him. She says that making this kind of decision takes time.

'What decision?' I say, not sure if it is to leave him or marry him.

'THE decision,' she says, rubbing her belly. I nod; neither of them then.

Camilla Rae reminds me of myself at times. At others, she is as alien to me as anyone.

We haven't spoken since the night we went swimming almost three weeks ago. Life sometimes gets in the way. That evening, a shoot of lightning zippered the sky. We were both in the water. I could feel it – through me. The ions or whatever you call them. Camilla Rae said, 'We're safe here.' I didn't know if we were or not. From what I'd been told, the last place you wanted to be was in a pool. She held her stomach the whole time.

Camilla Rae's hungry: she eats everything. Then she smokes. No one but no one is allowed to smoke in the store. She lights up anyway. 'I'm not no one,' she says. It dawns on me that if she were serious about keeping the baby, she'd find another way. She'd take up some other bad habit. Something that only involved herself. And then something else – that maybe this is just another way for Camilla Rae to keep Brad. 'Besides, you're the manager when the manager's not here. So relax.'

I can't relax. I keep thinking about the other Camilla. She cries so much in class I often feel guilty. I hear my mother in every word she says. I miss her. I hate her.

'You're not there yet,' Camilla Rae says. 'When you get there, you'll know it. It sounds horrible the way you described it. I'm not sure I could do it. But this guy – Saunders – he's supposed to be good. Right?' The idea of going back to class nauseates me. 'His books are everywhere. I thought about buying Brad one but you know how straight boys are. They'd rather drink beer and punch the wall and break their hands than look into the void. Everyone's got to stop running at some point.'

After Camilla Rae leaves, the day turns. Wind blows the tops of the trees back on themselves. Everything is coming undone: paper bags, empty cigarette packs, loose leaves, shingles from the roof of the hotel down the street. I think about class that night. We are getting closer to my turn to read. I think of Steven.

On my way home, I stop off at the Jolly Roger Fishery. Since class, life with Bob has become a kind of long drawn-out midnight. Where the clock just keeps chiming twelve. When he stumbles home now, usually around eleven-thirty p.m., I barely recognize him: I find scales stuck all over him like kisses. He no longer washes his hands before coming home or showers before bed. Bob's smell is powerfully nauseating. It is all I can do not to spend the rest of my life on the couch.

Sometimes, I even take a blanket and pillow and make a pallet for myself in the bed of his truck. Things you do in Galveston in summer. The best time is just before a storm, when the wind picks up and the barometric pressure drops to nothing in five minutes. Then you can lie there, with the world's fan blowing across your face, and drift into a tropical sleep.

'Hey stranger,' he says, wiping his hands on his blood-stained apron. Fish heads float in vats of seawater beside him. Lobsters claw their way up the side of a giant glassed-in cage. Their pincers make a clickety-click sound, like Bob in his sleep.

'Anything exciting at The Copy Desk?' he says, fiddling with the ice, rearranging the slabs of tuna steak.

The pink meat seems grey. Everything is grey without sun.

'Just a rerun of yesterday,' I say. 'And the day before that and the day before that.'

'We should go shopping tonight,' Bob says. 'We're out of everything.'

'Sure,' I say. 'After class.'

He looks at me again. I know this look of his. 'Then you're mine again,' he says.

'You never had me,' I whisper as he disappears into the walk-in freezer.

That night, instead of going to class, I head to Sears for a new ribbon for my typewriter. For the first time in several weeks, I do not feel like facing Camilla. I no longer feel hysterical; I no longer want to bite off my tongue. Thoughts of Steven, once unrelenting, have slowed. Now, they are simply background noise, like the rain. Each drop that falls brings me closer to sixteen again.

As I wander through the parking lot, I think of Camilla on her back, eyes riveted on the sodium lamps. I try to hear his name in the air. But there is only the rain. The police posted signs all over town: Have you seen this man? They haven't caught him yet, though they bring a new suspect in for questioning weekly. This according to Camilla, who visits the precinct just about every day on advice from Dr Saunders.

Inside, Sears is cool and dry and busy. Every aisle is packed with frenzied shoppers. Their faces are buoyant but terror-stricken; a hurricane draws near. Salesgirls rush around, like hungry seagulls. I find what I'm looking for almost immediately – a new ribbon for my typewriter. I have been down these aisles a hundred times. I forget to look for the boots. Maybe I'll give mine to Camilla Rae; a baby present. As I pay, I notice the clock above the doors. Dr Saunders has just released the class for their ten-minute break. I wonder which of us will eat the sandwiches tonight. I wonder if Camilla is weeping.

The rain stops momentarily, just long enough for me to make it home. The wind has picked up again. Other than this, the night is perfectly gaunt and still. While I wait for Bob to come home, his hands smelling of fish guts, I sit down at the typewriter. The blank page rattles slightly in the breeze. Each key echoes through the house, like our bed the last time we had sex.

Many years ago, when I first met him, Bob took me for a drive in his car, an old Chevrolet pick-up. He was a stock boy then. He said one day that he was going to trade in the truck for a more comfortable ride. I thought the truck fitted him. It was rough and needed a paint job but I liked it; it smelled safe. Only a man like Bob could get away with driving something like this, I thought. We drove down to the seawall, across from the Greyhound bus station. We parked and got out. Something was coming. The sea churned and the air held its breath. Like right before a storm. But it blew over and the last of the sun came out. It streaked the water and made it difficult to see. Bob asked me where I was from and I told him nowhere. We sat there, on the wall, in silence. He smiled and said that that was okay, that I didn't owe him a thing. It was funny when he said that because I was thinking to myself that if he asked me, I'd tell him I was visiting from somewhere else, like Chicago or New York. I'd tell him that I was in town shooting a movie. I told him that he was right, no one ever owed anyone anything, and the surest way to get hurt was to expect something for nothing. Sounds like you've been hurt an awful lot, Bob said. Believe whatever you want, I said and jumped off the wall and walked away. Where're you going? he called after me. I work at the fish market. That's where I'll be. The one with the guts all over his hands.

The parking lot of Food Heaven is full of cars. I stand outside the circle of blue-uniformed clerks on their smoking break and shoppers with heavy plastic bags full of ice. We are all impatient to leave; to get back to the safety of our air-conditioned homes before the food spoils and the ice melts. Being around all this food should make me ravenous. I'm not. I'm waiting to see my ribs.

Across the street, a pack of skateboard punks loiter in front of Dairy Queen. Some stand with their hands in the pockets of their acid-washed jeans, smoking clove cigarettes, setting napkins on fire. Steven used to take me to Dairy Queen for a Blizzard, while my mother was at work.

Bob comes out of the grocery store, clutching the rest of the bags. His face grim and dissatisfied.

'You could have helped,' he says, frazzled. 'The fat-arse check-out bimbo overcharged me for the damn eggs again.'

Bob is always fighting. Since I have known him, it is impossible to predict what will set him off. Sometimes, it only takes a penny. When we get home, I go straight into the bedroom, while Bob puts the bags of groceries away.

'I can't win,' he says.

'You were fighting with a teenager,' I say, fumbling in the desk.

'Can I read it when you're done?' he says, taking off his shirt, his pants. The zipper makes me jump.

'You already know this story,' I say.

He looks at me, fists raised. He thinks I am hiding love letters. He reaches down and yanks my chin with his hand. He kisses me hard on the mouth but I turn my head away. He can't get too close to me. Not now.

The night of our first class, Dr Saunders wrote a sentence on the chalkboard and underlined it several times. We read it silently to ourselves. *Violence brought me to this place.* Each one of us had to sign an agreement – no sex for the length of the class – but now I'm not sure that was such a great idea. I am torn: I want Bob, but I still feel Steven.

'Patience is a virtue,' I tell him.

'Patients are people in hospitals,' he says, putting on

his socks, then his shirt and pants. In his eyes are the steps that led him to me. His hands are bunched again into fists but on his face a smile persists. That smile hurts the most.

Bob uncurls his fingers, pressing them tightly against his sides. They are bloodless in the light, as smooth and white as paper.

'Bob,' I say, but he is no longer there.

I finish my homework on the typewriter and leave a copy of it for Bob taped to the refrigerator. I do not want to be around when he reads it. I have been through this before. Gathering my books and papers, I throw everything into my backpack. I do not want to leave Bob but I cannot stay. I tape another note to the refrigerator door. I love you, it says. Some things can't be explained by love.

I head out into August, the heat sticking to my skin. The sky cracks with lightning. I tuck the key safely under the welcome mat. This will make Bob insane. I imagine him driving around the neighbourhood looking for me. I imagine Bob will never believe in not looking for me.

The high school's parking lot is empty. Most of the windows have been boarded up. All in preparation for the hurricane. As I head to class, I remember my boots. I will have to go back for them at some point.

The room is dark when I go inside. No one is there. On the board, the word CANCELLED is written in chalk. I sit down at one of the desks. The air smells faintly of sulphur and smoke. Something I've never smelled before. Test tubes lie in neat stacks in the back of the room. There is a centrifuge, a scale. Camilla comes into the room and says, 'I didn't get the message either.'

She flips the light switch on but nothing happens. No fizzle, no nothing. Just the sound of the wind and rain against the glass.

'Maybe we should go,' I say.

Camilla goes to the window and turns around. 'Whatever happened to you,' she says. 'I'm sorry.'

I nod my head. Everyone is sorry. Someday soon, Dr Saunders will call me and we will meet for dinner to talk about it. He will write articles about me, about the boy in Galveston who told his mother what was happening with his stepfather, Steven, and when he did, she packed a suitcase for him and drove him to the bus station. How she sat with him until his bus arrived. 'You're going to stay with your aunt and uncle in Galveston,' she said. He'd never heard of any such aunt or uncle. She didn't believe him. She did believe him. Either way, this is where he is.

Camilla stands at the window for some time, humming quietly to herself.

'Do you need a ride home?' she says at last.

'Yes,' I say but neither of us makes a move to go.


A few days later, we are sitting on Camilla Rae's deck again. There is no music now, no smoking, no drinking, no candles. 'I feel bad,' she says. 'I went to my ob/gyn again. I can't keep anything down. Hey, don't look now.'

Headlights burst through the trees, angling across our faces. We both look at the same time, wondering. But we know who it is long before the lights dim and the engine shuts off. I have forgotten that today is a big day for Bob. That the new truck is the beginning of our new life together. 'When I get the truck,' Bob said, 'we'll take a trip anywhere you want to go, Glen.' I haven't seen my mother in years. It might be nice to see her.

'I should call Brad,' Camilla Rae sighs, 'to see if he's coming by later. I hate sleeping alone during a storm. Of course, he's probably out getting drunk. But that's what boys do I guess.'

'We could run away together,' I say into the wind.

'I wish we could go backward, you know. Even to a couple months ago when we went swimming. Remember? I wish sometimes that lightning'd struck me instead of the fence. I wish I hadn't gotten pregnant, I really do, but that's where I am,' she says.

Bob sits in his new black Chevrolet truck, the wipers beating back and forth across the glittering windshield. He honks twice. 'Glen,' he calls up as Camilla Rae heads inside.

'I'll call you tomorrow,' she says and kisses me. The deck creaks beneath her. 'If we make it through tonight.'

The wind is howling through the deserted streets. Everyone is indoors, waiting. In the distance, the waves break heavily against the seawall. A siren sounds from faraway, like a baby's cry. I think about what I want to eat. I haven't kept anything down in two days.

'Get in,' Bob shouts. 'It isn't safe out here.'

He's right. The sky breaks open and the rain comes. But it's not rain. It's hard and lumpy and cold. Bob starts to drive away, then stops. He honks again. I look into the apartment. I see Camilla Rae's feet dangling off her bed as she talks on the phone. There is Brad and there is the baby. I make my way down the creaking wooden steps. I look at the truck, at Bob. I climb into our new life and shut the door.

# music over fishkill pass

## 1

It was late in the afternoon and Flora Bloom – her real name lost like autumn petals; her favourite actress, Claire Bloom – sat in a booth by the window. The traffic along this part of Eighth Avenue stretched by, different coloured slugs slithering home. Madison Square Garden loomed like a spaceship off to her right, the main branch of the US Post Office across the street, regal and splendid with its colonnades. As she sat there, Flora imagined debutantes and their escorts ascending and descending the marble steps, an orchestra's lilting concerto within. The sight of the postman's creed filled her with a strange, indecent longing to be somewhere else. She didn't know why this was, only that it was. She felt displaced, sullen. It's because I never get what I want, she thought, as the cocktail waitress, a failed actress whose picture hung on the wall of Explosive Talent Acting Academy, set her sidecar down without a word.

Tedious and hot in the bar, Flora, sweating uncomfortably in her slinky black dress and nylon hose, kicked off her zip-up boots, the ones Cole, her fiancé, had brought up for her all the way from Austin. Sipping the drink, she fanned herself, thinking of him, when Buzz, her fellow thespian, walked in toting his duffel bag. They'd met two years ago in 'Realizing Your Breath', a class devoted to the Alexander Technique, and had been scene partners and friends ever since. That afternoon, Flora felt as sorry for Buzz as she did for herself, since it appeared he hadn't quite mastered his character.

After ordering his beer, Buzz dropped into the booth, eyes riveted to the television in the near corner. A man in safari get-up, a thin mesh covering his face, stood against a flat landscape, the sun setting behind him. Mountains rose toward a purple sky and sapphire dragonflies swarmed around him. He held a net in one hand and in the other, an unlit kerosene lantern.

'This is the best time of day to catch them,' he said with an Australian accent. 'Because by morning, most of them will be dead . . .'

Flora glanced at Buzz intermittently, while she sipped her drink. Such an attractive man, she thought, with his hard mouth set into an angular, meaty face. His natural talent as an actor usually overwhelmed her and she found herself daydreaming about going to bed with him. The problem was, Buzz was homosexual, although when he'd told her this, Flora had shaken her head in disbelief. Now, sitting across from him, she believed him even less.

Something in Buzz was so extraordinarily masculine, she thought, the way he moved, the manner of his voice and deportment. Her own brother, back home in Dallas, was homosexual, a real flamer. When she'd visited last year, he'd seemed even more so, the lisp having become more accentuated, his gestures, the flick of his wrists, the swish in his walk, more exaggerated. Under some

162

suspicion Buzz wasn't exactly what he said he was, Flora wondered if placed in the right situation, he might not be swayed. She thought of that single moment last month during their scene when Buzz leaned into her, his breath a mix of coffee and something else, sweet and delicious, and kissed her. He'd fainted; she'd nearly swooned.

'Did I tell you,' Flora said, 'about this guy that came into Morton's last night? I think the universe is working a little magic for me.' Flora was big on the universe, on synchronicity. A long-ago winner of a Miss Teen Texas Pageant, she spoke with the slow deliberation of a girl raised on wide, friendly spaces and wild, sudden storms. 'All suave and debonair, shelling out fifties like business cards. Just the kind of guy my mother wants me to marry. Anyway, it turns out he works for William Morris and wants me to come in for an audition next week.'

'That's great,' he said, though she could tell he didn't really think so.

'I know what you're thinking,' she said, 'but he gave me his card this time and everything seems, well, legit.'

Flora had been through this routine before, many times in fact. She'd gone on one audition after the other and usually left feeling good, if not slightly cheapened. Was it her fault she'd inherited her mother's chest and luxurious black hair, her father's dimples and smile? And she wondered what these men saw — or rather hadn't seen — in her to ask her in for a first meeting but never a second.

'So, why don't we go over that scene again?' he said.

In the waning afternoon light, Buzz reminded Flora of Real Auger (yes, that was his God-given name), who was supposed to have met her at the bar an hour ago. An acting teacher at SUNY-Purchase, she'd met Real while auditioning for the lead in his revival of *Saint Joan*. She hadn't landed the part, but as a consolation prize, he'd taken her to dinner. She'd been carrying on an affair with him ever since.

'Oh, Buzz,' Flora said, looking down at her watch, tapping the face to make sure it was working. 'There's no rush. We have weeks to practise. You just rest, and try not to worry.'

'Are you waiting for Cole?' Buzz said.

Flora shook her head. 'Like always,' she said.

What could she really tell him? That asking Cole to move from Austin to be with her in New York had been a wild and impetuous mistake? That something had flickered and died the moment he'd set his cowboy hat and guitar in the bedroom? That she felt awful for disrupting his life, but in proportion to the disruption he was causing her, she wished he'd drop dead?

She hadn't yet told Buzz about Real, wasn't sure how he'd handle it. She knew from experience he struggled with some sort of moral dilemma around exclusivity and love. That his loyalty was the crux of his problem, all of his problems. 'Sometimes, you simply have to call it quits,' Flora said absently and realized by the expression on his face, blank and eerie, that she'd spoken at all. 'I mean, right?'

They ordered another round as the lights of Eighth Avenue snapped on and the traffic thinned into taxis, not much else. Every once in a while, a cab sped by and Flora's heart dilated, and then she wanted to jump in it and take it as far out of Manhattan as she could get.

'So I've been meaning to ask you again,' Flora said, feeling a little sloppy after three drinks, 'about this weekend. Can I borrow your apartment while mine's being repainted?' Oh, she hated to lie, hated the words as they left her lips but what else could she do? She was a woman in love with another man or was it something else, something more dramatic?

'Yeah, sure. I'll be in Fishkill,' he said.

'With Davis?' she said hesitantly.

Buzz shook his head. 'No Davis,' he said.

Three weeks ago, there'd been warm candlelight, mussels, a bottle of Domain Chandon, all paid for by Davis, Buzz's drug-addled boyfriend. Unfortunately, the night had ended with fisticuffs at the table, which then escalated into a full-scale war on the street. They'd subsequently been banned from the restaurant.

Outside, a taxi came to rest at the curb and there was Real, looking piqued and stressed, the fringe of his face boiled and red. He was shouting at the driver, banging his hands against the Plexiglas divider. Uh oh, Flora thought. As Buzz rummaged around in his backpack for the spare set of keys, Flora held out her hand impatiently and said, rising, 'Well, maybe Cole and I'll surprise you on Sunday. He should be done with the painting by then.'

'Sure,' Buzz sighed, taking a sip of his drink. 'See you later, Flora.'

Flora rushed from the bar, just in time to grab Real and another taxi but not before Buzz had turned his head, gave her a strange, if not knowing, glance and then went back to watching TV, his face saddened somehow by what he'd seen.

Through the deserted streets of the Meat Packing District, Flora held her breath. Even though it was late in the day, an unseemly odour hung in the air. Traces of chicken and pig parts swirled in puddles along the curb. Flora nearly stepped in one but Real yanked her aside just in time. A couple of feathers stuck to the sole of her zip-up leather boot. Like most New Yorkers, she hated summer. A transvestite paced up and down Little West 12th. She wobbled unsteadily on her heels, casting shadows on the metal gates of the abattoirs.

They arrived at Buzz's apartment, sweating. Flora was no longer in the mood for a love-in, but Real had come all the way from Purchase. She shuddered with guilt, appraising Buzz's hot, ramshackle apartment. Throwing Real down on the futon, just drunk enough to get away with it, she said, 'I want your cock inside me.'

'You make me feel so cheap,' Real said, smirking, undoing his zipper.

When Flora saw his cock, she wilted. Why am I about to fuck a man who didn't give me the lead in his stupid play? She pictured Buzz on the bus, drunk and alone, making his way to the country. 'Maybe instead of hanging out in this sweltering dump, we'll surprise Buzz tomorrow,' she said as Real, who registered nothing, drove his way into the hole of her being.


# 2

As the cab pulled into the driveway, Buzz was startled to find all the lights on, the stereo blasting a Sibelius concerto, and smoke unfurling from the chimney. Davis, he thought, angry and relieved, as he walked through the door and into the house he'd rented for them. He dropped his bag and backpack to the floor, the air chilly. It amazed him how different the temperature was just an hour-and-a-half's drive from the city. Fifteen degrees cooler. Fall had already staked out a life in the trees, gilding the leaves.

'Davis?' he said. 'Davis?'

He drifted upstairs to the empty second floor, with its three bedrooms, the twin beds neatly made and pillows exactly in the same spots. The house was too large for two but Buzz luxuriated in the space anyhow, loving the many rooms to wander into and out of. His studio apartment in Manhattan barely contained his claustrophobia.

Downstairs, he went to the deck to check on his flowers, the petunias and gladioli and hibiscus, which the deer kept nibbling on. And there was Davis, seated in one of the chairs, smoking a cigarette.

'You made it,' Davis said. 'I'm glad.'

From here, Buzz thought he caught the twinkling black eyes of a deer, but when he looked out, the copse held nothing but pines. The air was thick with their scent, and that other smell, which radiated off Davis, familiar and sticky sweet. He sighed and settled in beside his boyfriend of several years, both teenagers when they'd met on vacation in Spain. Now, at twenty-five, Buzz wondered exactly what he'd seen in this boy who still slept with girls, who'd served such a mean ace and drank pint after pint of Dos Equis, as if trying to impress him. He'd fallen in love with Davis that first afternoon on the clay courts, and had kept it up through an ocean and years of separation – Davis in Switzerland at a private boarding school, Buzz, a few years older, in Manhattan at NYU.

'I made it,' he said, resting a hand on Davis's warm, hairless arm.

The intense heat of his skin made Buzz flush and turn away. He still loved this boy. The maelstrom of their love had brought them here, to this retreat in Fishkill three months ago, where Buzz had hoped to reach some sort of tenable armistice: shuttling Davis out of the city, away from 107$^{th}$ and Broadway – Heroin Hall. Davis, ingenious and industrious, found heroin anywhere, even on the loneliest dirt road.

'Want to go swimming?' he said. 'I've been heating the pool. It should be ready by now.'

'Not tonight,' Buzz said, letting his hand slip away.

Davis rose, his body ungracious in the sweatshirt and jeans. He moved in front of Buzz, and stripped. His pudgy, white body glistened, marmoreal and unreal. Not a body of extraordinary lines and muscle, just natural, fashioned from years of tennis and water polo and skiing. He was bright to the point of brilliant, subtle to the point of deceitful, gentle to the point of fragile. Buzz knew he wouldn't hurt anyone, unless he had reason, turning this violent streak inward, upon himself instead. He was self-destructive and selfish, a terrible combination.

Buzz wasn't naïve enough not to believe that his loyalty to Davis held a trace of the self-destructive as well. That, after years together, the best thing would be to leave him permanently. But he just couldn't bring himself to it.

He reached out his hand, uttering softly, 'Come here,' which Davis did. He slipped onto Buzz's lap, wrapping his arms about him, and as they kissed, Davis was fourteen again and Buzz had just discovered another country.

In the morning, amid the first autumn breezes, Buzz went out to tend to his garden. He thought of Flora and Cole awakening in his tiny space. He puttered in the dirt, yanking weeds and tossing stray stones that had somehow found their way into his carefully planned rows of lettuces and peppers and squash. The hurricane fencing had held this time, and he marvelled at the tracks the deer left in the soft earth around the perimeter. Scavengers. The door to the deck clacked and Davis stood there, dunking a teabag into his mug.

His dark hair hung in his face, but even so, Buzz could just make out the red-rimmed eyes, and even redder lips; Davis was high.

'Thought I'd go into town today,' he said, his voice thick and slurred. 'Anything we want?'

'Maybe some more, um, condoms,' Buzz said.

He thought he heard Davis grunt. 'Like we need them,' he said, pivoting and walking back into the house. Through the screen door, he added, 'I'm taking your wallet.'

Buzz spent another half an hour in the dirt. A pack of deer stuck their wet black noses out of the woods, stock-still, surveying. Buzz rose, clenched hands into fists and said, 'Go on, get the hell out of here.' The deer tore off, leaving in their wake shimmering leaves.

Inside, he fixed a pot of coffee, but there was no cream. Gone as well, the bottle of vodka, and all the other assortment of sweets – Snickers and Milky Way bars, Milk Duds and Butterfingers. Davis. Jesus.

Beyond the house, a car turned into the gravel drive and Buzz bristled. The police again? He went to the window and saw the blue Impala, Cole and Flora in the front seat, speaking quietly. With every drag she took, the tip of Flora's cigarette burned with a muted intensity. They were arguing, a speciality of theirs. The way it had been for ages, since he'd met her two years before. She was always in this state, either of provocation or ambush.

Flora climbed out of the car, thin, bony arms jutting from her sleeveless sundress. She flew toward the front door, a winged insect, her mirrored sunglasses reflecting everything in miniature. Cole sat there, aggrieved and put-upon, the fine bones of his fingers clenching and unclenching the steering wheel.

'Well,' Flora said, her voice adrift on the late morning breeze. 'Let's get it together, Cole.'

Buzz's heart sped up. First Davis and now Flora. He'd come here to get away from the tragic heat and absolute chaos of summer in New York. Away from the crowds and the stinks and the reminders of his static acting career. More important, he came to get away from himself. Now, with Flora and Cole here, Flora, whom he'd suspected was having an affair with Real Auger, a man he personally disliked for having told him once, after an audition, that he should hold onto his day job, he'd never find peace. At Flora's knock, something inside Buzz crumbled, and he raced upstairs for his pills.

He hadn't felt the need for them until then. Davis who came with his habit and Flora who wouldn't let him forget she was moving on and up, while he was being left behind. All at once, Buzz detached, floating through the empty bedrooms, each piece of his body taking a different bed. In this scattering, Buzz found relief, and swallowed the pills.

Flora's knocks rose through the house, louder each time, her insistence like the woman she was. She'd always get what she wanted; beautiful girls always did. She'd sleep with dozens of boys without consequence; Cole, stalwart Cole, would keep coming back. Cole's loyalty outshone his own and as he padded downstairs to let Flora in, Buzz felt the whirl of the world, some great dark pinwheel spinning in his head, and he slumped down to the floor and shut his eyes as the migraine bloomed.

## 3

From the front seat of the Impala, Flora turned to Buzz and said, 'Are you feeling better?'

Buzz shook his head and said, 'Yeah, a little. Thanks for helping me to the car, Cole.'

Cole smiled, nodded. He'd hefted Buzz about the waist, carrying him to the car. Cole's body full of a strength Flora hadn't realized. Buzz must've weighed, what, twice Cole? Cole, who stood five-feet-seven, and came up to her chin. But there was something gigantic about him, redoubtable. Is this what attracted me in the first place? His singing? The songs he wrote? Flora wasn't sure anymore.

'What brings on a migraine?' she said. 'The cold?'

'Not sure,' Buzz said. 'It'll pass. But I really should get my prescription refilled, at the pharmacy.'

He'd collapsed on stage last month from a migraine directly after they'd kissed, that moment of such heat and intensity even Flora had felt faint, ecstatic she'd finally inhabited the whole being of her character. Living in the sorrow and pain, Real had said once, is only half of it. The other half is figuring out how to cope once you're there.

Flora's way of coping, by flirting and seducing, often left her feeling like an underpaid whore. She blamed the beast, the movie biz, with its casting couches and informal drinking lunches, the redwood Jacuzzis, the air jasmine-scented and electrified. For a while, Flora had only wanted to deal with women, but they seemed even more suspect than the men. Meaner, more critical. At least with the men, she got a free dinner. She wondered then how she'd had the stamina for it, going from one office to another, hopeful and giddy, only to leave heavy-hearted.

'Neither rain nor snow nor heat nor gloom of night,' Flora said, twisting in her seat. She climbed in back, while Cole fiddled with the radio, music suddenly filling the car.

They came to the road that would take them into town, Main Street, with its ice cream shops and kids on bicycles and pizza parlours. The air smelled of burning cedar, the plumes of which hung feathery and soft against the distant hills.

'We had the nicest drive up here. Didn't we, Cole?' Flora said, touching his shoulder, catching something shift behind his spectacular brown eyes.

Cole nodded, turning right past a field of freesia. She stared at Buzz and there it was in his face, that knowing, as if he could see right into her skull. She shivered a bit, folding her arms about herself.

'Not much traffic on the Deegan,' he said. 'Okay time. A lot better if someone hadn't forgotten to buy gas.'

'Cole.'

'I'm not saying it's your fault,' he said, good-naturedly, waiting for a car to cross the one-lane bridge out of Fishkill. 'It just missed your mind. Like not buying toilet paper or kitty litter or food for the weekend.'

'We can get food at the Shop Rite in town and besides, you only work part-time. You could've done the shopping.' She paused. 'You managed not to forget your guitar,' she said, more to Buzz. She rolled her eyes.

'I'll just be a minute,' he said, shutting his eyes.

'Does the light hurt? Is that it? Do you want sunglasses?' Flora said, as if speaking to a child.

Buzz tilted his head back, his Adam's apple sharply pronounced against the thin skin of his throat.

'Well, I'm going shopping,' Flora said, and with that, she left them there.

In Shop Rite, Flora grabbed a cart, skating up one aisle and down another. She loved the sense of order each can and box offered. Rows of pasta, cereal and rice, jars of hearts of palm and salsa and vegetables in their briny, pickled sauces. She pulled things off the shelves. It didn't matter. She was in Fishkill with Cole and Buzz and things were definitely looking brighter.

She skidded to the check-out line, where Davis was speaking to one of the cashiers, a high-school girl with pigtails and splotches of acne across her limpid forehead. A policeman stood by, his eyes going from Davis to the girl and back again.

Flora had never liked Davis. She'd called him out the second their eyes had met. Bad people always recognize each other. She saw Davis for who he was; a leach and lothario, who made Buzz's life insufferable. She hoped Davis couldn't talk his way out of this, whatever this was.

But then, she heard, 'accident', 'pocket,' 'never again', and then she watched Davis walk out, grinning, the hole closing up behind him.

'The most talented actor of us all,' she said to the cashier, who crinkled her nose and smiled artificially.

When she returned to the car, Cole and Buzz were in the front seat, Davis in back. Buzz said, 'Look who found us, Flora.'

The air smelled hopeful and sugary. A brown paper bag rested between Davis's legs, spots of whipped cream on his lips. 'You didn't tell me Davis was going to be up this weekend,' she said. 'Nice to see you.'

'Likewise,' Davis said, smirking.

Davis dropped his eyes to the bottle of whipped cream, moved them to the window where dusk was settling. The lights of the shopping mall flickered on. In the distance, the landscape swelled into a thick black mass. It was frightful how easily night enveloped and obliterated. An artery of lightning stung the sky. Thunder sounded the approach of a storm.

'So how's Real Auger, Flora?' Davis said.

'Real Auger?' she said, alarmed, staring first at the back of Buzz's head and then down at her nails, the cuticles unkempt, the muted tangerine nail polish chipping.

'Yeah, Buzz said you kissed him in a cab yesterday,' Davis said, the grin widening until all his teeth showed. 'I think he's pretty hot, for a has-been.'

'Davis,' Buzz said. 'Shut up.'

Cole fiddled with the volume on the radio as the car filled loudly with acoustic guitars. Flora moved as far away from Davis as she could get, moulding herself to the door. She rolled down the window, stuck her face out, the wind refreshing and pleasant. So there it was.

She hated disappointment, but such was her life, another skin that stretched beneath this other. This world that had been hers, its hungry ambition, minor success and countless sorrows, which Flora felt just as surely as she felt her bones shatter. Please, let a car hit us, but Cole kept to his lane and the others to theirs and then they were back at the house.

Flora leapt out. Bleary-eyed, she ran upstairs. Nothing would be the same, and who she was and where she wanted to go seemed as unmatched as two different socks. She didn't have it in her and yet, as she moved to the twin bed, she felt as if she'd stopped acting, as if until that moment in the car, she'd seen her life on a screen, one-dimensional and detached.

She'd been with Cole for nine years, had met him in college as a freshman. He'd seen her through two abortions and one miscarriage, the death of her father, pneumonia and ovarian cysts. But what he hadn't seen her through was her desire to be more.

She heard Cole on his guitar, his voice rising like the sweet and tangy aroma of smoke blowing in through the open window. She listened to him, the inflections and subtleties, this man she felt so much and so little for anymore. It's horrible when love dies, but isn't it worse pretending that it hasn't? Stretching out on the bed, Flora shut her eyes and waited for Cole's ballad to finish.

# 4

Buzz awoke the next morning to the sound of percolating coffee and the sizzle of bacon. The air, crackling with grease, smelled woodsy. He lay in a sleeping bag in front of the fireplace, the ash sifting through the grate, picked up by a rush of chilly autumn air. Standing up, he went to the deck, remembering the night before.

A lone buck pranced around the yard, stopping to gnaw one of Buzz's petunias. 'Get lost,' Buzz called. The buck, not completely convinced, nibbled at one of the purple flowers. He just stood there, in awe, appalled – the hours and weeks spent in the dirt, plotting the bed, digging through the layers of shale and clay, removing weeds, tree roots, flint and glass.

Through the kitchen window, Buzz watched Davis, spatula in hand, hovering over the griddle, a mound of bacon and pancakes on a plate beside him. His movements were swift this morning, far swifter than last night when he'd caught Davis and Flora making out on one of the twin beds upstairs.

While swimming, he'd come to some minor epiphany about love and need, their incompatibility. The rain hadn't yet fallen, though the air contained all sorts of wicked possibilities. Cole had sat on the deck, strumming, moving his mouth without singing, eyes shut. Buzz had wandered past him, the sound of the guitar as sorrowful as he felt. Upstairs, he'd heard a murmur, a sigh, a squeak of the bed. That discreet sound of kissing.

'Caffeine?' Davis said. 'Sleep well?'

'Bad dreams,' Buzz said through the screened window. He felt his mouth surer this morning. He'd made some great decisions in sleep and was ready to set them out: he wanted Davis gone, Flora and Cole on the road by noon. 'Someone's arm got chopped off.'

'Castration fantasies again,' Davis said, face with minute red splotches.

Buzz turned toward the yard to see the drooping limbs of the trees and the scattered, broken twigs. The fence surrounding his plot sagged noticeably.

'Davis,' Buzz said, 'you have to go.'

Davis dropped the spatula in the sink and met him on the deck. He stared at Buzz askew, kissed him hard on the mouth. 'But you love me,' he whispered and kissed him again. 'Doesn't that count?'

Down below, at the pool, Buzz heard splashing,

176

Flora's alto, Cole's baritone. He took a step to the edge of the deck to see her pointing at something, her face shadowed in the fall sunshine. Up above, the silkiest blue Buzz had seen in a while, as if the storm had wiped away all of yesterday's smudges.

'I know you hate the bus, but I'll buy your ticket,' Buzz said, feeling Davis's heat behind him.

He turned around to find Davis in a completely unflattering red Speedo. In the full light of morning, his love handles and stretch marks saddened Buzz unaccountably. How hadn't he noticed, or cared, that his lover had put on so much weight? He knew love's burden, its pull and fascination, its unkindness. Is it possible to find someone attractive one moment and loathsome the next?

'Let's skip breakfast and have some old-fashioned fun upstairs. Let me get rid of Flora and Cole. We could have the house to ourselves. Like we used to,' he said, a wild desperation to his voice.

'I want you out,' he said, moving toward the pool, stopping to inspect the damaged petunias. He met Cole halfway.

'I wouldn't go down there,' Cole said, sandy blond bangs dark with water and hanging in his eyes. 'She's in a mood. Lost one of her contact lenses. You know Flora and her eyes . . .'

'Listen, Cole,' Buzz said. 'I'm sorry about Davis. I really am. He had no right to say that.'

'It's all taken care of,' Cole said, his brown eyes drifting from Buzz to the woods. 'Wow, look at that.'

Buzz pivoted, following his thick index finger, which pointed to a family of deer, six in all, grazing blithely on the sweet dewy grass. 'Jesus,' Buzz said.

'Pretty courageous animals,' Cole said. 'Beautiful and

simple. Wish everyone was like that,' and with that, he drifted back up to the house.

At the pool, Buzz watched Flora swim the butterfly, her movements quick and sure. He stuck his feet in the water. Flora stopped in mid-stroke and swam to the side, shaking drops from her thick, black hair.

'We need to talk,' he said.

'You need to keep your mouth shut, Buzz,' Flora said, climbing out. She stared past him to a motion of branches, a footfall deep in the woods and added, 'Cole's going. He left it up to me, like there's any decision to make.' She paused. 'Why'd you do it? I mean, it's not like I told Davis about your infatuation with Cole. But then again, you guys have that kind of weird, kinky relationship so I guess it wouldn't matter anyway.'

Suddenly, Buzz felt as if he were sixteen again, that he'd never escaped the torturous confines of high school. 'Flora, I don't care who you sleep with or why,' he said. 'But you involve other people and you just don't care. How many guys do you need, Flora? How many?'

Flora laughed. 'We're not rehearsing "Hedda Gabler", Buzz, so don't patronize me,' she said. 'You should be having this conversation with Davis, not me.'

'I'm not infatuated with Cole,' he said, approaching her, fingers splayed and rigid at his sides.

He'd known of Davis's dalliances for a while, his casual, if not meaningless, flirtations. He'd always suspected Davis of infidelity, of transactions made in the dark. The phone calls at all hours of the night from random men and women, the wad of cash at the back of his sock drawer (Such an unoriginal place, Buzz had thought), the tiny amber vials he kept in the medicine cabinet next to his prescription for Retin-A. There were also weeks of such sweetness and love that somehow balanced out, even negated, all that had come before them. Not anymore. He'd kissed Flora. He felt real terror then, stark and precise, the incision of teeth along his spine.

Angry, he said, 'I knew one day we'd come to this. Was he good, Flora? Did you like feeling Davis inside you?'

'Yes,' she said, irises dilated. Then, 'No, not really.'

And he understood something more – that it wasn't Davis she'd been after. He'd suspected this when they'd met two years ago, when she'd walked right up to him after class and said, 'I can help you.' She'd stood too close, eyes too focused on his face, lips. And then of course there was that kiss during one of their scenes, a scene that required no kissing.

They were face to face now, Flora and Buzz, two actors without roles, two people leaving and being left. Buzz stared into her eyes, two different colours without the contact lens, one green, the other boring blue, and he laughed. He'd never known this about her, that her eyes were flat and ordinary. Nothing wild about them.

'Flora,' Buzz said softly, his tongue and fingers tingling.

'You deserve so much better,' she said, reaching out a hand to touch his cheek or to hit him, Buzz couldn't tell.

As her fingers struck his face, Buzz felt the muscles in his arms slacken, a dark, unbridled energy surging, and he rolled forward. The last thing he saw before hitting his head was a look of uncomplicated satisfaction slipping over Flora's face.

the storm had come, knocking out the phone lines. It had shaken the windows and rattled the cedar shingles until the house seemed to give up and come apart. Buzz and Cole had slept soundly through the storm, which had only lasted fifteen minutes. While it raged, Flora had fucked Davis.

A cool prickle of air rushed in through the screen door. Flora followed it out into the white lash of light that fell onto the deck. She listened for Cole, gone and not coming back. Davis lit up again and offered Flora the pipe. She'd never smoked heroin before, and for reasons she herself was unaware of, she took the pipe and sucked in. The world turned dense and fuzzy, as if she were looking at it through a prism. She realized then she'd lost both contact lenses and that her spare set, along with her glasses, was in Cole's glove compartment.

Listing down to the pool, where Buzz still lay flat and motionless, she lifted up his head gently and touched something gooey and wet. 'Oh my God,' she said, staring at the smears of blood in the grooves of her palm. 'Buzz, if you can hear me, I want you to know,' she said with panic, and stopped. She wasn't sure what she wanted him to know.

Buzz made no signs of listening; his eyelids remained shut. Flora rushed back up to the house, calling Davis's name, her voice like the warble of some great bird bound for extinction. When she got to the deck, Davis had vanished, taking the plate of bacon with him. Flora stumbled inside, called out his name again. Nothing.

'Unbelievable,' she said, tripping out the front door.

The air gripped her, clean and overwhelming. The storm had felled weakened limbs and swollen ditches. Water ran in shouts along the side of the road. She thought of Cole, careful, abiding Cole, who'd left his life in Austin behind to be with her. But it had been a different Flora he'd encountered upon his arrival, no longer the ordinary girl from an ordinary town but someone with sparkle and shine. Who'd changed her name, dropped twenty-three pounds, and hungered.

Flora set off quickly, marching, head cocked and alert, the muted autumn sun her only companion. She'd heard stories of these back roads, of wild beasts, UFO abductions, cults. In an hour, perhaps less, the sun would set and the woods would blacken, changing what had been into what would be. A few minutes later, something sharp pressed into the sole of her foot. Flora winced, the pain excruciating, and she was forced to stop. As she dug the sliver of glass out, she remembered her part in *Saint Joan*, as one of Joan's allies. An incidental role.

A crackle of footsteps, a shiver of leaves and Flora froze, fearing the worst, a band of wild dogs, wild kids, rednecks. She closed her eyes. She was alone, nothing to stop the wind from startling her. When she opened her eyes, there was simply what there had always been: the road, burning cedar, the lustrous eyes of the many grazing deer.

She pictured Cole crossing back into Manhattan, and then into Brooklyn, where they lived in a modest one-bedroom apartment over a pizzeria. Cole, who'd sung to her that morning, 'You can't always get what you want but sometimes, you just might get what you need.' She sighed, and broke into a gambol, still hearing Cole, still tasting the sweet and tangy smoke.

# 6

The patrol car arrived at the house, while Buzz sat on
the deck, reading a back issue of *Variety* by flashlight.
The power still hadn't come back on, the phone, still
dead. The painkillers were taking their full effect,
erasing the throb in his head. He'd left the Scrabble
board out to finish his game with Davis, the words
taking on a different weight the longer he stared at them.
He remembered a game he'd played long ago with
Davis, an avid Scrabble player. Even high, Davis had
beaten him by over three hundred points.

He'd recognized the genius in him then, and something else, a beguiling slowness, which he'd taken as
calm, but now, saw as plain old apathy. Buzz hadn't
always worried about Davis. There had been months
when it seemed Davis had left his habit, that he was as
ordinary as any nineteen-year-old. Flipping through the
pages, Buzz felt the descent of worry all over again, that
one day he'd get a call, a deal gone awry, or worse, an
overdose. Buzz wondered, jumping at the sound of a
voice, deep and male, issuing from the front of the
house, if he'd been too impetuous in asking him to leave.

Heading to the door, he pictured Davis on the
Trailways bus that would take him back into
Manhattan. He loved Davis, but love couldn't possibly
fix him. Buzz knew this, just as surely as he knew the
further Davis receded, the better off he was. He couldn't
afford him any longer, nor felt the need to be held
further accountable. The kleptomania, the heroin, the
bingeing, all of it had taken on a life of its own. He was
sick with Davis's indifference.

When Buzz opened the door and saw the cop, hat in
hands, face cast down, he understood. For a moment,

standing there, he was all set to identify the body, to make the necessary arrangements. He'd been rehearsing this for years, the moment he heard.

'Mr Buzz Welch?' the cop said flatly.

Buzz stared past him to the patrol car, the red and blue sirens whirling, their light reflected into the leaves. In the darkness, Buzz surrendered to the idea of eminent bad news. 'There's been an accident,' he said. 'Could you come with me, please?'

In the front seat, Buzz stared out at the cyclopean wilderness, the occasional beams of a passing car. They drove with alacrity through these shambling back roads. Buzz thought about Flora, how, in her struggle to be a renowned actress, she lost that which made actresses great. The ability to distinguish between the art and the craft, how you inhabited the character and how that character behaved in your skin. The problem with Flora was that she had no character of her own, that she'd compromised the essence of who she was for the promise of who she might be. She lived in the almost.

The cop shut the sirens as they glided toward the bridge that would take them into town. And there it was, the discord of the accident, a formal production of sparked flares and ambulances, bystanders on the periphery, whispering, wondering. Another cop in a neon-orange jacket diverted traffic from the bridge. People gawked from their porches. Kids on bikes rode as close to the scene as they could, pointing, eyes wild with disbelief.

Buzz stood there, taking in the blue Impala, the front end buckled around one of the bridge's steel suspension girders. Through the shattered windshield, he made out the crumpled figure of Cole, head cast back, as if asleep.

The guitar case jutted out through the missing passenger-side window. He shuddered.

'We found your address in the car,' the cop said. 'The boy's hurt bad, but nothing a few days in the hospital won't fix.'

He kept on talking, but Buzz no longer heard him. Spotting Flora, who was moving toward him, her face gummy and expressionless, he shook the tears from his face. This wasn't part of their scene, part of the people they were. He'd no idea what he was going to do.

Turning to the cop, Buzz said, 'He came back,' more question than statement. 'Cole came back for her.'

## 7

Flora wasn't sure where she was or why. She listed through the crowd, feeling numb and disoriented. All this was relative. She often felt this way, on stage, in her real life, with Cole, and there was Buzz, speaking to the policeman and the Impala on the bridge and she took a step and then another, floating on blistered feet. Flora passed the policeman in his neon-orange jacket, the flares like dynamite, glass everywhere, people chattering, assuming. She heard words: 'drunk', 'idiot', 'tragedy', but registered only the sound of her own heart, rumbling like mad in her ears. She heard music.

And then she was at the car, the radio announcer's voice, then more music, music on the bridge, while someone shouted at her and someone else grabbed her by the shoulder, but she fought him back, enraged and delirious. She dipped her hand through the window, not looking at Cole, his mangled body, the spears of glass in his lap, his head snapped back, the vein at his neck throbbing imperceptibly. A one-man accident. She set the guitar on the ground and fumbled for the glove compartment, the little door on the floor among maps, pens, cigarettes. Flora drew out the case, which held her contact lenses, so small in her hand, and the glasses, the plastic frames oddly intact. She placed the glasses on her face and suddenly, the world snapped back, glistening and unreal, and Flora let out one terrible sob.

Buzz was behind her now, hands on her back, leading her from the wreckage, away from Cole, stupid, lovely Cole. How could she deny it now? How could she ever have? Everything there: the car pointing in the wrong direction, the direction toward the house, not away from it. And she knew then he'd been coming back for her, the only reasonable explanation. She turned to Buzz, his face smeared and wet.

Gently, Buzz took the guitar from her, leading her away from the smoke and the noise and the horror of her own culpability. And Flora held onto her friend's hand, the kindness in his fingers like warm alchemy, renewing, if only briefly, her faith in their hard, cold world.

# a few words about my son

Taking it in slowly, I let it all settle while he tells me about my son. The sun rollicks through the windows, tiny white slivers of light that catch the stains in the carpet, which I've been meaning to clean for months. I'm no good with these things, and usually Sally, my lady friend, intervenes. She's a beautiful woman, Sally, kind and generous, even if she is a little too heavy for my tastes. Who am I to care? I'm not the track star I once was. No one is what he once was.

On the phone, he's saying, 'Mike left his body to science,' and in the background, I hear the faint whistle of a kettle, or is it a siren? 'Mr Lowenthal? Are you there?' he says.

Am I?

I'm down in all that dirty shag doing push-ups, ten, twenty, thirty, heart fizzling like a faulty electric socket. After a hundred, I rise, trembling, a map of tensile blue veins levitating up and down my arms. I jog in place, while the idiot's saying, 'Hello, hello,' into the air, persistent like that. Not knowing. Then I sprint to the hall closet, timing myself: eight seconds, good.

'I'm here,' I say, my voice on the other end in New York.

I'm vacuuming up lint, dust and Sally's cigarette ash. Later, I'll be in the basement examining the new sander (the carpet hides beautiful blond wood) I bought yesterday at Home Depot. I'm anywhere else, anywhere than in my house, while this man, this roommate of Micah's I've never met, though have heard about (haven't I?) tells me that my son is gone.

I know I should ask him the inevitable question, the one that forms and dies inaudibly on my lips – how did my son bleed to death? But my voice chokes and the question stalls.

'I'll book a flight. Thank you for calling,' I say and hang up, realizing I can't remember the roommate's name.

When Sally arrives with our usual Wednesday night dinner – spinach lasagna, a salad of iceberg lettuce and tiny grape tomatoes, garlic bread – I'm curled up on the couch, face in the cushions. Not asleep, but not awake either. From the kitchen, Sally calls, 'Jesus, David, I've been phoning you all afternoon . . .' One, two, three steps and she's in the doorway. I don't move, or rather, my grey matter refuses to cooperate with my body, and I let out a single sigh.

I'm not a crier. I haven't in years, not when my mother and father were taken in a freak and inexplicable car accident when I was in college, not when my sister, Cathleen, died of lung cancer four years ago, not when my wife, Micah's mother, left me last year. The only time I've cried – and this must say something about me, though I'm not sure what – was when I held Micah in my arms. Those first few seconds.

'David, are you all right?' Sally says, her voice full of the tender insolence I've grown to expect and admire.

The smoke from her mentholated cigarette settles in the chintz, the carpet, the curtains. I've told her a million times I'd rather she didn't smoke in the house, but at this moment, I don't care what she does.

'I give up,' she says and I listen for the soft tread of her heels.

I am a solid piece of driftwood, carved over time by the crush of sand and sea. If I could move my limbs, if I could just lay my stoic blue eyes on Sally, I'm sure things would be okay. I can't move and so, after a few minutes, I hear the sound of cutlery shuffled, of ice tinkled into glasses, of plates dislodged from the cabinet. Little domestic nuances.

When I finally awaken hours or days later, put my fifty-eight-year-old body through its circadian rigours, my neck sore, my arms numb, there is a plate covered in tin foil on the coffee table and a note, *Is this what life with you is going to be like?*

Ravenous, I eat the lasagna, the wilted, acidulous salad, the soggy garlic bread. Then, I go into the bathroom and vomit into the toilet, which, like everything else, needs a thorough scrubbing.

WE LIVE IN A FAT WORLD. SO TRUST YOUR GUT. JOIN GOLIATH GYM – AND LOSE. I see this billboard as I drive to the airport the following morning. I own Goliath Gym, here in Buffalo, where I'm something of a local celebrity given the ads that air frequently on TV and radio. Maybe you've seen the ad – Micah and I in matching tank tops and shorts, lifting dumb-bells, while stills of my son flash across the screen.

'This is me before,' a nineteen-year-old Micah says,

indicating a shirtless fat boy with round face and double chin. 'And after,' at twenty-two, lean and muscled. 'I couldn't have done it without Goliath Gym. And you, dad.' I smile, cup my son round the shoulders. 'Let's hit the whirlpool,' I say, and we fade to black.

That spot cost me three months' rent to produce, but was well worth the effort. Membership soared, yet, in the last couple of years, business has tapered off considerably. It's hard to compete with the chains.

Our plane doesn't depart for hours. Pragmatic if not punctilious, I like to sit and watch the travellers, kids with their stuffed elephants, mothers with their lipsticks, fathers with their newspapers. People-gawking, this is certainly a trait Micah and I shared, if I can say anything for certain, if I can say anything about my son.

I check our scheduled departure against the finger-smudged, greasy-screened monitors: two hours, ten minutes. In two hours, Sally will bound through the electric doors, reeking of smoke. She'll be wearing what she normally does – a navy-blue sailor suit, with shiny brass buttons and pleated skirt. Her flying outfit, she calls it. The same suit she's worn on every one of our weekend jaunts, to Las Vegas, Carmel, Denver. If I'm the King of Punctuality, then Sally is the Queen of Jitters. She hates flying, always has, it seems.

Yesterday, when I called to thank her for the lasagna and tell her about Micah, she said, 'Oh, God, David . . . Oh God,' and then she broke into fits of uncontrollable sobbing. 'I'm such a petty bitch. That note I left. Oh God.' She'd only met Micah a couple of times, at my fifty-eighth birthday party, at the celebration of Goliath Gym's twelfth year in operation, at Thanksgiving last when Micah showed up an hour late, without his roommate, Henry, grumbling about men and unpredictable moods. Yes, of course, I think, as the shadowy gangway swallows up a solitary man. The roommate, Henry.

In the gift shop, I poke around the books and magazines. And there is Micah, on the cover of *Playgirl*, his hairless (hairless?) stomach muscles hard as enamel, his smiling face more handsome than mine ever was or could be. I see his mother in his face, in the angles and fine indentations about his mouth. The thick, fluttering eyelashes, the absent, grey eyes. For a moment, I'm at his first Little League game, when he missed every single pitch, and the other boys on the team corralled him, drawing a menacing circle tighter and closer. I watched this happen from the fence, fingers clenched in the wire. I said nothing on our ride home, nothing to take the wicked sting out of his shame.

The clerk says, 'Would you like a bag, sir?'

'That's my son,' I say, pointing, convinced this has some meaning.

The clerk, a fine enough looking young man, tents his dark brows and nods. From the strange glimmer in his eyes, I know he doesn't believe me. Sure, he's thinking, sure it is. And then I'm sliding Micah away, pixel by pixel, into the sack, first his feet, then his torso and then his sweaty face, until every inch of him is concealed.

Sally and I met several months ago in the basement of Grace Church. We were there for the bi-monthly meeting of SOCAL (Supporters of Children with Alternative Lifestyles). My wife had been a member for years, ever since Micah had divulged his homosexuality to us.

I said, 'This doesn't change the way I feel about you,' but in secret, I'd prayed he'd come home to tell me differently. My wife went to SOCAL, alone, because I simply couldn't bear what I pictured going on in the basement: the whining, the why-me's, the blaming. It seemed my wife couldn't commiserate enough with the other parents. I didn't see the issue. So our son's gay. So what, I told her, each time she asked me if I wanted to go. He's your son, too, David, she'd say, less scolding and defensive than disappointed.

After she moved out, I thought about joining a group for divorcés. But all those weepy men? Instead, I showed up at SOCAL one evening. I suppose it was my way of taking up some memory of my wife, her ongoing struggle despite me. (I still loved her, but as she'd said that final morning, 'I don't fault you *per se*. You were just a little boy. How could you have known about your crazy, fuck-up of a sister?') Going was also a way of cajoling myself out of the house. Then, it didn't seem to me that my attendance had anything to do with Micah. I'd just lost my wife of twenty-two years. Who could blame me for wanting some company?

At the time, Micah was living in Manhattan and though we spoke often enough, once every couple weeks, our relationship felt strangely formal, as if we were meeting again after a prolonged silence. I don't believe Micah didn't want to talk to me, but after the divorce, something between us shifted, like the quick movement of a storm. And with it came a wall of rain, which further blurred him to me, although his voice always made it through. There was a looming disconnection, a click, minute yet omnipotent. It made me feel as if I'd done something dreadful. Hadn't I?

That first evening, I sat in the circle with all the other parents, some married, most divorced. It wasn't my intention to fixate on Sally, but there she was, outspoken and boisterous, saying things like, 'We just need to understand them better!' and, 'If they can't turn to us, who else can they turn to?'

Sally's own son, Clark, had been beaten in an alley outside a bar in downtown Buffalo. He sat beside his mother that night, sullen and listless, a moody boy with the same intrepid posture, flat back, rigid shoulders. Bruises ringed his silver-blue eyes. He was missing a tooth. It didn't seem likely to me he'd been the victim of what Sally called a hate crime. He was big and burly, six-feet-three with large, pan-sized hands and a deeply commanding voice. And I wondered then, what sort of man was ambushed like this? What sort of man was Clark?

I thought of Micah, just as tall yet less redoubtable. Could something like this have happened to him? Would he have put himself in such danger? For certainly, Clark had deserved this flogging, parking in a deserted alley, walking to his car alone at three in the morning. My son was too smart for such nonsense, I found myself saying, and, before I could shut my mouth, I'd made enemies with just about everyone there, including Sally.

'What does his sexuality have to do with it?' she called to me from across our circle. 'I'll tell you, Mr Newcomer. It has EVERYTHING to do with EVERYTHING. So please, the next time you want to join in, think before you speak.'

Ten minutes up, we hit turbulence, ten minutes into that soaring blue. During which, Sally clutches my arm, her nails leaving faint grooves in the skin. 'Talk to me, David. Tell me about Micah,' she says.

And so I tell her about my son: about his strenuous birth, the umbilical cord wrapped around his neck, the time he was three and fell off my shoulders, about rushing him to the hospital, his head gushing blood. I tell her about when he was nine and found his mother and me playing used-car salesman/prospective buyer naked in the garage. The camping out on our bedroom floor from ages eleven to thirteen, after I'd mistakenly taken him to see *Invasion of the Body Snatchers* (at his repeated request, because, as he said, 'It's just a movie, dad'). The first time he kissed a girl, Lynn Carr, behind the tool shed in our backyard, the last time he kissed me goodnight, at fifteen. The years of straight A's, the battles with his weight, thin to fat, the trouble finding him suitable clothes. The bulimia.

I tell Sally about Micah and as I do, he becomes less my son, more a boy, a boarder, who lived in my house, ate my food, slept in the brass bed I bought him for his twelfth birthday. He becomes the detached arms, words and face of any stranger who's made little or no impression in the room. The compilation of details, at once too real and too vague, to make sense to me. As we head closer to New York, I realize something: I can't wrest the moments of my son's childhood from my own.

Up in the air, I forget Sally is just my lady friend, that we haven't been together long. That Micah isn't gone, that there will be no funeral, not even a remembrance. In a way, I'm glad for this. In a way, I'm saved from having to say a few words about my son.

Here is Queens, there Manhattan, the skyline, buildings and traffic. Why would anyone willingly choose this place? Why, Micah? I'm stymied.

Sally smokes, her fingers trembling. She sits with knees squeezed and face locked on the window, which is cracked slightly. 'Second-hand smoke kills, too,' I say softly as we drift away from La Guardia. I'm trying patience, levity.

On the ground, things take on a different depth, coloured grey with failing afternoon light. My hands are liver-spotted, my skin cragged as a tree trunk. In the rearview mirror, I catch my face, creases of time in the forehead, around the eyes. I'm ageing at an alarming pace here in the backseat. I think of Micah, half my age, gone and never coming back and then all the mysteries, the secrets he kept in that skin of his, the bones of his skeleton.

It is Saturday afternoon and the traffic light. We make it to the Chelsea Lodge Hotel on West 20$^{th}$ Street with remarkable speed, or so says our Armenian cab driver. Sally leans in and whispers, 'Tip him well, David.' She kisses me on the cheek, and for a moment, everything is as it should be, except that we aren't here on one of our weekend jaunts. We're here to collect and carry away my son's possessions.

Once in the room, Sally uses the bathroom, while I call Henry, Micah's roommate. As I dial, I count the number of years they've been living together. One, three, four – he answers on the third ring, says, 'Are you at the hotel already, Mr Lowenthal? I hope you like it.'

'Very historic,' I say, though one hotel room is just like any other to me. 'It's great, really. Terrific.'

'I guess you'd like to come by to . . .' Henry says and pauses. 'To, I'm not sure, I got some boxes and trash bags.' There is magnificent strength and sorrow in his voice, and an unexpected softness, which throws me off. So different from that other voice, the voice on the phone yesterday, with its finality and detachment, as if he'd made the call a million times already. All of a sudden, I am struck that Henry may be someone else, someone more to Micah than simply his roommate. Not that it matters, because it doesn't. Not really. But I have to know. It's the details, the particles of dust that float and settle, watering the eyes.

'Henry,' I say, as Sally flushes the toilet and the door to the bathroom opens, 'you and my son were more than roommates, correct?'

Sally sighs, lights a cigarette, the room filling up with her. She hangs behind me, her pelvis smooth against the small of my back. I feel discomfit swell and deflate inside me, something white-hot and red-centred. 'I loved Mike,' Henry says and then rattles off his address, their address. 'You're very close, by the way. It shouldn't take you long.'

After I hang up, dazed, Sally says, in one of her more insolent moments, 'What did you think, David? You need to brush up on your euphemisms. I mean, talk about the Dark Ages.'

As we walk from the hotel to West 22$^{nd}$ Street, hordes of young men stroll past, clean-cut, good-looking men in tank tops and shorts, though it's far too cold for such clothing. I think of their fathers, what they might say if they could see their sons like this; the vaunted, whorish display. Because it seems to me that's exactly what they are. Whores. They stand singly and in pairs, glancing first at my crotch and then lingering on my body, muscular if not more so than most of theirs, than most men my age.

In their eyes, I detect wonder and confusion: Is he one of us? For a moment, I lose myself, as Micah must have lost himself, in what seems like another world, without women, without their plotted domesticity. With Sally beside me, there is the slow, renewed distaste of where we are, and why.

196

My distaste: it's something Sally and I have discussed over the last few months, something that arises every so often in those bi-monthly meetings. You hear so much about diseases and unsafe sex and the drugs and the alcohol. As a parent, I wasn't as horrified to hear stories of gay men and their promiscuity as I was saddened by it. What kind of men were these? I wondered. What exactly went wrong?

On the way home from one of our meetings, Sally said, 'Some of them have over five thousand different sexual partners, David. Some have even more. It's no different, gay or straight. Men are men.' Wasn't it different? Isn't it?

I learned later Sally was speaking from experience: her own son, Clark, had contracted HIV in the mid-90s. He'd told her a condom had ruptured. How did she really know? We only have what our children tell us and if they're really our children, they'll lie as we lied: to maintain our distorted vision of them.

All of a sudden, I stop, ashamed, and grab Sally's hand. I kiss her, displaying an unusual affection. Me, who dislikes this sort of fanfare; this unnecessary, albeit sweet, intimacy.

I say, 'I love you, Sally.'

'Are you all right?' she says, drawing back, not so much stunned as incredulous.

I want to tell her: I'm not ready, never been ready for this. That I should outlive my offspring. That I'm scared, because I see Micah everywhere. I think of the magazine stuffed deep inside my carry-on. I want to tell Sally about it, more about Micah, the adult he became. But I don't know what kind of adult he became.

'Never mind,' I say.

*

So the facts: Henry and Micah were indeed a couple. I find pictures of them together in Micah's room (and their office), on the desk. I search each drawer, but there is only the usual – bank statements, computer disks, old letters from his mother, the odds and ends of any life. The bottom-most drawer is locked, which doesn't surprise me.

As a boy, Micah kept a metal lock box in his closet, full of bits of quartz, a BB gun he wasn't supposed to have, a slingshot, broken and irreparable, an arrowhead. I know this only because I discovered the key. What is surprising to me is that Micah hid things even from Henry.

The key: If I find it, what then? What nasty secrets will I discover? Searching the room, I hear Henry and Sally, their voices rising and falling through the closed door. There isn't much else here. A throw rug, dusty and worn, an old framed poster of *The Big Sleep* (Who did he like more, Bogart or Bacall?), a trophy on a bookshelf from 1976, when he won second place in The Bicycle Rodeo at Larkspur Elementary.

He was eight years old, a roly-poly kid with thick brown bangs and a thicker waist. I see him on his blue Schwinn, with the banana seat and orange fibreglass flag. He hated that flag, the idea that his dad didn't trust him.

'It's not you I don't trust,' I said, attaching it. 'It's the other guy, Micah.' This wasn't actually the truth. I didn't trust him. He'd already disobeyed us, pedalling too far from home, as if he were attempting an experiment, to see how far his little legs could take him. That afternoon on the bike, weaving around the bright orange pylons, steadying the bike on the thin yellow rail of a line, I saw something beautiful in my son. His determination and attention, the fervour in his grip to hold the bike on its course. Not to fall, to swerve. I thought, Here is my boy and say whatever you like, he's going to make me proud. And he did. He brought home that trophy and we celebrated with pizza and ice cream and then we took him to the drive-in to see *King Kong*. It was a fantastic night.

I think about that night in particular because it seems to me the beginning of something and the end to something else. Micah changed drastically after that. His tantrums increased in size and pitch; he grew sullen and irascible for no apparent reason; he put on more weight. My wife wanted to take him to see a child psychiatrist, but I wouldn't hear of it.

'We can handle our son,' I said. 'This isn't leaving the house.'

I often relate Micah's change to that trophy, because really, after that, nothing went well for him. I imagine he must've been under the spell of winning, that rush of adrenaline that comes from good luck. We can only hide behind our trophies for so long before they are put on the shelf and forgotten. Which is exactly what happened. I put Micah's little trophy on the mantelpiece, and went back to my life.

Now, dumping the dusty trophy in the box, I wonder, why am I here, sniffing around this room? A jealous wife riffling through her husband's desk for love letters. What do I expect to find? There is greed and hunger in the process, something too natural. I try the locked drawer again. Locks are something else we had in common.

When Sally knocks and then steps sheepishly into the room, I'm sitting on the floor, exhausted. My eyes moist, my nose twitches with dust.

She says, 'Henry wants to take us to dinner. Are you hungry?'

I turn my eyes to her and suddenly, I miss Micah more than ever. I want him back. I want that day back, I think, and my anger swells until my fingers bunch into fists and then uncurl, splayed out, absently attacking the comforter. I want my son back, I'm shouting, but Sally can't hear me because my lips don't move.

Sally leaves. I hear her say, 'Yes, we'd love to. Just give David another few minutes, okay?'

At Viceroy, on the corner of 18th Street and Eighth Avenue, we have to wait outside until a table is ready, but, as Henry says, 'It's really worth it.' As we stand there and Sally and Henry talk about the rise of HIV infection across the country, I'm somewhere else, adrift, watching the men parade up and down, jolly and, dare I say it, gay. Sometimes, there are women but mostly not. Gathering around us, in clumps of threes and fives and sevens, I have to wonder who they are, this onslaught of men who resemble one another, from the shape of their facial hair to the exact style of their Nikes. None of them is fat or out of shape. An army, I think. Some even sport fatigues.

Henry spies me staring and rolls his eyes. Leaning into me, he whispers, 'Welcome to Stepford.' An inside joke apparently.

One of the men, bald with earrings and thick moustache, fifty years old if a day, approaches Henry and says, 'Chuck will be in Nova Scotia for Mike's bon voyage so he can't make the memorial, but rest assured I'll certainly be there. We all will,' and with this, he motions to the entirety of this spectral army clotting Eighth Avenue.

Like a woodland creature sensing fire, Sally draws my hand into hers, and squeezes. A friendly squeeze, something else lives in it as well. The smoky lust of loneliness, a determination to see us through. I will underestimate Sally for as long as we're together.

Henry turns to me, lower lip slightly rouged, and says, 'I forgot to mention . . .' but before he can finish, the bald man interrupts. 'Chuck and I are just horrified about what happened to Mike. Henry, you may have a law suit on your hands.' He slides my son's roommate a business card. 'Call me,' and then he turns back to his friends, with a subtle nod to Sally and me.

The food is brought out, served with a flourish by our waiter, who says, 'Bon appetit!' I look down at my plate, at the curried mango chicken, my stomach clenching. Sally dabs her burger with ketchup, glances at me and says, 'That looks yummy, David,' as if speaking to a child.

With methodical care, Henry chews each bite of his blackened red fish. The dangerous thread of bones, the undetected remains left in the fillet. I make it a practice never to eat fish that I myself haven't caught.

I devour my plate of chicken and rice and mango chutney and it actually tastes good. The first real meal I've eaten all day. I'm used to going without food, mostly out of forgetfulness. It's a funny habit. ('Not funny ha ha, David,' said my wife. 'Funny weird.') It's important to remain fit, to draw life out to its most conclusive end.

Swallowing his last bite of fish, Henry says, 'Mr Lowenthal, there are some things I need to make clear . . .'

'Maybe later,' Sally interjects, but this is too

201

important to wait until later. Later, I may not be here. Later, I may be hunting. Later.

'Tell me,' I say, resting a hand on Sally's. She fidgets uncomfortably, and under my touch, nothing but concern. I'm glad you're here, I think. So very glad.

Drawing the napkin from lap to mouth, Henry says, 'Mike and I took care of each other, and I think that's the most important thing. I loved – love – your son, Mr Lowenthal.' He pauses. 'This is difficult. I don't know how much you know.' Another pause. 'Mike wanted the liposuction and he made appointments and consultations without my knowledge. I couldn't talk him out of it.' He pauses again and searches the room as if Micah may walk through the doors. He shakes his head, in defiance or sadness, I can't tell. 'This place can make you crazy if you let it get to you,' he says. I suspect he must mean the men, their gaudy, seductive displays.

I turn to Sally, whose face goes liquid in the dim light of the restaurant.

'Will you both excuse me for a minute?' I say, rising. More than rising, floating, and then I am down in the bathroom. There is the mirror, reflecting back at me this old-man face, with its crevasses and meaty chin and ill-begotten ears. As I wash my hands, my son slips across my face, a fugitive shadow, and I turn away, toward the stalls.

Slipping into the space, no larger than my closet at home in Buffalo, I slide the latch shut. This takes effort, what I am about to do, the focus of fire. I think of all the tiny misgivings, the aches and subtle pains of childhood. The memories: of that sharp throb below my navel, that compression of breath by some unseen hand, those moments I was convinced of a heart attack – all this before the age of twelve. I remember my own father, the physiologist, and what he used to say: 'It's all in your head, boy.' Was it? And my mother, later, in the darkness of my bedroom, her cool hand on every uncomfortable point. 'There,' she'd say and, like some saint, smooth it gone. Had she?

Over the porcelain bowl, the clean bluish water, the hint of lemon disinfectant, I inspect my middle finger. It was my sister, Cathleen, who showed me the grace of the middle finger, who taught me her magic one evening, while our parents fought.

Even now, as I kneel beside the toilet and glide this finger past the uvula to the back of my throat, that moment lives again, briefly, when every ache and sorrow, every grief and disappointment evaporates. It only takes a second. While I disgorge the contents of my stomach, there is a wonderful silence, a calm like no other. How beautiful to have this much control.

It is difficult in this moment not to think of Micah, of that time long ago when he accidentally found me in the bathroom.

'Are you feeling bad, daddy?' he said, standing there in his pyjamas, holding a doughnut.

It was a Saturday morning and in the background I heard the TV, cartoons, the coyote and the roadrunner, one in constant pursuit, the other in constant flight. My wife, Micah's mother, was in the kitchen, doing the breakfast dishes. And there I was, on the tiled floor, throwing up the eggs and the toast and the oatmeal. I could've been sick. I told myself I was.

'Are you feeling bad, daddy?' Micah repeated, face blanching with worry. 'I'll get mommy.'

I flushed the toilet. I said, 'Yes, daddy's not feeling too

well,' taking my son around the shoulders, perhaps too gruffly. 'But let's not bother mommy right now. I'll feel better soon.'

How can I explain it to you, Micah, what your father was, and still is? I'm not stupid enough to believe that what I do is normal. Or that it won't someday lead to serious consequences. What I didn't know then, and what I do now, is how, in that one minor miscalculation – not locking the bathroom door – I think I may have bequeathed something to Micah, something far too heavy for him to hold. I see his face again, as it was that morning, the disapproving lines around his mouth hardening, gravity suddenly made manifest; the mysterious will of a child. He just knew.

'I won't tell,' he said, offering me a bite of his lemon-filled jelly doughnut. And he didn't, until many years later.

At the table, Sally sits beside Henry, her wallet out. Pictures of her son, Clark, in front of her: Clark as a boy in the choir, as captain of his Little League team, dressed as Joe DiMaggio. I've seen these pictures already and, as I sit down, Sally hastily folds up the wallet and replaces it in her purse, saying, 'Do you feel like some dessert, David?'

And I'm laughing, not at Sally's question but at the way we slide between worlds, the secrets we keep. How not less than five minutes before I was hovering above the toilet. What secret is Sally keeping from me? Because isn't that the true nature of love, protecting each other from our wickedest parts?

'If we're going to make that memorial in the morning, I'd like to go back to the hotel,' I say.

*

Driving home after that first meeting in Grace Church, I cursed myself for having gone and swore I'd never go back. What did I need with a bunch of malcontented parents? With a guy who turned to me at one point and said, 'I'm not surprised your kid ran away.' What did they need with me?

A few days later, the phone rang and when I answered it, I was startled to find Sally on the other end.

She said, 'I know it's none of my business and I'm sure I'll regret having this conversation later, but I just need some clarification: Are you really as backwards as you seem to be?'

I couldn't help laughing, which made Sally laugh as well. What could I tell her? I read a book a year, I liked to fish, made a decent living. I hunted deer and wild turkey, had never raised a hand to my wife or child. Yet, there were stirrings inside of me I couldn't explain, strange slants toward violence, judgements before the fact. Damage. Insolvency.

'I recognized you, you know,' she said when we got together later in the week for dinner. 'Goliath Gym. I always told Clark, "Those two are the handsomest men in the county." Clark always agreed.'

'Thank you for the compliment,' I said.

It was the first time I'd been out with a woman since my divorce. I wasn't sure how to behave, whether to force my charms or let them sit in back, simmering. I thought of telling Sally about my wife, thought against it. There would be time for this, I hoped. We were at that age, when time speeds up, when you glance at your watch and it's hours later, not just minutes. I was having a good time.

'It's too bad Micah doesn't live here,' Sally said, grinning. 'I think our kids would probably hit if off.'

'I don't know,' I said, returning the grin. 'I haven't the foggiest.'

After a bout of terrible sex, Sally says, 'Maybe I should have my saddlebags sucked out.' She is sitting up in bed, tiny buttons of sweat glistening on her consternated face. 'Maybe you'd enjoy fucking me then?' She moves into the bathroom, rippling as if I've just dropped a pebble into the centre of her. Through the door, she adds, 'And maybe I'd enjoy you more if you liked touching me.'

'Sally,' I say, 'that's not it.'

What can I tell her? That the sight of her naked doesn't repel me as much as it reminds me? 'What the hell am I doing – with you – acting like Florence Nightingale?' she says, returning, hairbrush in hand. 'You. Invited. Me.'

I have no idea what I've done. I didn't call out my ex-wife's name, I didn't say an unkind word. Yet, I suppose it's all in what I'm not saying that offends her.

'I just lost my son, so fuck off,' I say, weakly, as if this can explain away the last thirty years of my life. I am calm and in my calm Sally finds further offence.

'Yes, you did,' she says, softening, climbing into bed. 'But you say it like you're telling me the moon's out.' She pauses. 'I already know the moon's out, David.'

I shake my head, lie down beside her, shut off the light. I'm not a talker. I come from that generation of men who had our feelings tailor-made, by parent and country. What is the use of talking about how I feel when nothing is how I feel?

Hours later, I open my eyes to find Sally naked and snoring, her hair bunched around her face. The TV on, the large square screen casts its Neptune blue through the room. Ten storeys below, the night traffic shoots up and down the avenue.

206

In the bathroom, I wash my face in the dark, eyes shut to the eyes in the mirror. I switch off the TV, and squat at the foot of the bed, watching Sally sleep. The skin of her thick arms droops, freckled and mushy, one of her breasts peeks out from the sheet, nipple hard. Cellulite drifts and clings to her thighs. Not that long ago, she would've been called voluptuous. Today, women like Sally are called large, plus-sized. Fat.

If it is possible, the sidewalks are busier than before, buzzing with packs of men, young and not so young, smoking and chattering and showing off. Here is Micah's world opening up to me again, how he saw it and how it saw him. I think of the SOCAL mothers and fathers, my ex-wife who will arrive in the morning, and the drive out to East Hampton, where the memorial will take place. Henry Bell has arranged it, our limousine, the flowers, the music, the catering. It was an unexpected announcement, this memorial, and so, as I make my way from the hotel to Micah's apartment, I think of what I will say, the synopsis of my son's short life. What stories to impart to these men, who seem more like orphans in this inhospitable world. Where are their fathers, the moral divining rods, my generation? The faces of these boys, younger and younger, smashed up against the sides of the street, hemmed in, this ghetto. I see Micah everywhere, the sharp lines of his face, the brown-amber eyes shaded green in summer, the cleft chin, the broad bow of his back.

I buzz Henry; I need information. I want to know what went wrong. I want to hear the story of my son's life and I want Henry to tell it. I will not leave until my father's sense of righteousness has been assuaged. I am in a slow, ungenerous sinking.

The intercom scratches and the lock clicks and then I

am up the stairs and on the landing and then, just as I am about to knock on the door, a boy shrugs by me and it takes a moment to realize this boy is Micah. It is not unheard of, sightings after the fact, intentional disappearances, coincidental evaporations. When you've tampered with the body the way I have, it is common to envision, hallucinate. I know this is exactly what I'm doing, out of fatigue, emotional and physical, out of the breadth and scope of my grief.

The desk and Henry can wait.

Light-headed, I plunge down the stairs after him, quick as he is, and back out into the street. My heart feels unbolted from the rest of me, a shambling, clunky muscle. Micah's mother used to say I'd never die from a heart attack because I didn't have one. This was toward the end, when I gave her every gut punch and treachery. I deserved her wrath, everybody's. I'd somehow managed to mangle my insides so that everything I said came out garbled. A distant, dead language. I thought my wife could help me decipher me.

He travels quickly down 22$^{nd}$ Street, trailing dozens of trios and quartets, a stream of older men in chunky military-style black boots and tight jeans. The younger men, like Micah, wear the latest Nikes and looser-fitting dungarees. Some sprout baseball caps. Most are clean-shaven. They are narrow-hipped and well toned, or so it seems. When naked, I imagine them putting most women I know to shame. There is a ravishing about them, an essential shimmering cloud of childishness.

Micah moves swiftly across Ninth Avenue and veers right. The wide lanes hold taxis and SUV's, an occasional ambulance, the telltale sign of misfortune. I hurry to keep up with my son, the black streak of his head as it joins another tangle and then separates smoothly, quicksilver.

He hastens right, a toy soldier in shiny black leather. The night cool off the river, the wind etches these stone caverns and waters my eyes. Micah pauses in an unlit doorway. From where I am, at the corner, I can almost hear the flint, his diligence to make fire. The wind eases and there is smoke, an orange eye in the gritty dark. Behind me, the New Jersey shore rears up in leonine splendour.

The crowd fans out like blooming hydra, a thing with a thousand arms and heads, everyone packed near a particular portal lit by a single blue bulb. A giant clot of a man, bald and purple as a prune, wields a sceptre, its end fastened with a shrunken head. Stringy hair, toothless, grinning. The black door swings wide to swallow an anointed pair. Others push and prod the velvet rope, but the doorman goes unswerving in his stony divinity. He chooses two from the middle of the crowd, two young men with bleached-out eyebrows and pink Mohawks. Gawks and sneers rise and die away. The two punks make their way inside.

In a black leather jacket festooned with a billion silver paperclips, a boy hands out postcards to this, CLUB NARC (short for Narcissus?). Many cards lie abandoned on the pavement, oily sneaker treads blotting the solitary image of a man's ribbed abdominals. If I didn't see it here before, I see it now; this silent communiqué of commodity. And there is Micah, swift and beautiful, stationed among them, yet decisively apart. He slides to the rope, which parts quickly, and disappears into the warehouse. Right before the door closes, I swear I see him turn around and wave.

*

In Grace Church, I learned about the lives of urban gays, that particular variety of men who left behind home and family for New York. I heard repeatedly about their random meetings on the street, the subway, in bars. Sally recommended books so I read up on my son's life. The public bathrooms with holes carved in the walls, deep-shaded groves of bamboo, an abandoned pavilion, hunting in Prospect and Central Park on bright summer days. The author wrote in liberating flourishes, something in their need for danger made it beautiful, he said. Maybe it did. I read everything, gay magazines, books, newspapers. I had to wonder, as I sat with Sally and Clark, this mother and son, if things might not have worked out differently if I'd just told Micah once, all those years ago, while we'd fished, played catch, painted the house, that I liked him. That at times even I felt desperate, for who I was and how I was and the world hadn't yet choked off that part of me that could've saved us.

An hour later, I am chosen and move along the shrouded darkness of the hall toward a line that ends at a ticket booth. A thin man-woman with a single false eyelash perches behind the Plexiglas window. Twenty-five dollars later, I wait in another line, the coat check. There, men strip down to nothing, shorts, underwear, less even. All of them, no matter their age, remove shirts to exhibit the personal diary of their bodies. The eerie machinations of vanity. Inhuman bodies. Every one hairless, tattooed, bronzed under the lights. For a moment, I think of checking more than my coat, as if to understand Micah truly I must shed more layers.

Another oblong corridor and the main chamber, one city-block long and two storeys high. The music punches through me, rattling my rib cage, the cartilage of my nose. I'm not the only one who's dressed, yet I feel suddenly naked, scrutinized. What am I hiding beneath my clothes, inside my jeans? This is what the eyes wonder.

I am here for my son, I think.

As I progress around the perimeter, the heat turns radiant and I'm wet almost instantly. It is a tropical heat, of jet streams composed of sweat and breath and the sear of dancing bodies. A few women lounge, sip pink drinks out of martini glasses. One ties a cherry stem into a knot with her tongue. I am surprised to see them, relieved actually, and want to join their clique, speak of the natural world beyond these walls. There is no time for that, and I slide away from them, their squeaky laughter a shrill resonant above the deep bass of the house music. (We play similar music at Goliath and although I dislike it, I care more about my clientele's repeated patronage than about their musical tastes.)

A huge mirrored ball reflects odd rosettes of coloured light – yellow, green, blue, orange, red – onto the waxy wooden floor. Slowly, it makes sense: I am standing in an ancient roller-skating rink. The dance floor shaped like an open mouth, the lips the railing. In the centre of it all, there is Micah, his shirt hung off a belt loop, his body a memory of my own.

I think of his mother, the way she danced around the house when she thought she was alone. I think of Sally, asleep in the hotel, and how much I'd like to be with her. Micah spins and swirls, finds the nearest body, and presses himself against it. They are unmatched, in size and height, Micah far too tall, this stranger far too wide. Yet, they dance with even gaits, graceful, the curves and slants of their parts finding equanimity in the other. When they pivot around, there is Henry, the roommate, though this seems incredibly unlikely and I laugh. My stomach is hollow and anything here is possible.

As the song merges and blends, Henry, eyes teacups in his face, unravels from Micah, and heads toward the bar. There is no kiss, no intimacy left between them; they've burned it off in the fury of the dance. Micah rebounds immediately, already in the arms of another; and their circle closes, the lights go out and the music shifts abruptly. Some dancers decelerate, many still race and rock, gyrate to an internal, drug-high glissando. Someone blows a whistle, a calling for what? A warning?

Arms and hands joust the air, reaching. Here is Micah's true family, I think, all these men, thousands of them. They paw at my son, his thin musculature, the jeans, his only clothing, until he's finally exposed, the outline of his sex visible through the thin white cotton briefs. Is that ecstasy or panic on his lovely face? Are the hands raised in defence or allure? As I push hurriedly through the dancers, I feel something, a jagged peak rising into a familiar and warm terrain of disgust. Life spins under the spell of lights.

'Let's go, Micah,' I say into the wild, febrile air behind him. The familiar whorl of his big ears, the swirling bristle of dark hairs along its spongy, pink ridge. Several moles line the soft expanse of his upper shoulders, his back smooth and unblemished, no thick hairy wings, no sign of his Semitic heritage.

Micah pivots around to face me, his horsy brown eyes loose and wandering. He looks me up and down, not like a son but a consumer, gauging the bins of produce for freshness. He doesn't recognize me or, if he does, pretends not to.

'Baby,' he says, drawing as close to me as he can.

'Dance with us,' and then stalks around me, bumping hips.

'Get dressed, Micah,' I am saying but my words are murdered by the music. 'I'm taking you home.' I pick up his discarded jeans, moist in my fingers and hold them out. 'Put them on.'

I unbutton my shirt, the men watch me, faces questioning. My body is sleek and firm, the hair on my chest curly and grey. One man reaches out to stroke it but with a quick snap on the wrist, I disabuse him of the gesture. He seems bewildered and enraged, as if I've broken some commandment. While I'm wrapping a strangely pliable Micah up in my shirt, Henry Bell returns from the bar, wielding two cocktails, his handsome face deflated and friendly at once.

He says, 'Mr Lowenthal?' and thrusts a cocktail at Micah. 'What are you —'

'We're going home,' I tell him and he nods, backs up and away, until he's nothing more than another body among the dancers.

In a darkened corner by the coat check, I help Micah into his jeans one button at a time. His stony eyes shut for seconds at a time and he's mumbling in some exotic language, Yiddish maybe, though I'm not sure when he learned it. We've never been out of the country, but maybe it's time to go.

The jeans secured, his own shirt tucked in, we wait for the girl to bring his coat. I tip her five dollars and she says, 'Happy Birthday to you, too.' After which I carry my son out of this place and into the cold electricity of morning.


TRUST YOUR GUT. I came up with that. Goliath Gym – that was Micah. He'd just read about David and

213

Goliath in Hebrew school and was obsessed with the story.

'And since your name's David,' he said one night in his bed, 'it just makes sense.'

Yes, Micah, it did make sense then to call our gym Goliath, as if the world could be broken down into men and giants. But the world on that crisp morning doesn't seem as simple to me, feels suddenly vaster than it has ever felt. And I wonder how it is I have confused physical and internal force, how much harder it is to slay the giants when they are our own failed marriages, our own trapped and disappointed lives, the things we learned long ago that have become written.

I lead Micah to the Chelsea Lodge and on the way we stop off for coffee and cinnamon rolls, flowers for Sally. I devour two rolls in the elevator, while Micah sips his coffee, black, no sugar, the rouge of his cheeks the surest sign of life. On the third roll, I decide that it might be better to save it for later, when I'm truly hungry.

'You keep calling me Michael,' he says and in the sudden light of the hallway, I see his face clearly. A tight approximation, yet this boy isn't mine.

'Micah,' I say and spell it out. M-i-c-a-h.

'He must be pretty sexy,' this boy says. 'I'm Sean, from Duluth. Are you just visiting or do you live here? Lots of people live here, you know,' and then he kisses me on the cheek. 'You're really hot, for an older guy.'

My face goes fiery, the rest of me icy and numb. 'Thanks,' I say.

Sally is still asleep when we slip into the room. Sean says, 'Hey, wait a second,' as I turn and lock the door. Sally awakens, calls out my name. Yes, I think, yes, and for the first time smell the smoke on my skin.

My son lies on the floor beside the bed.

Sally sits up, speechless, not so much confused as oddly moved; I see it in her face. Her breath catches and before she can speak, I can tell she sees what I saw, this boy's peculiar resemblance to Micah. Sean walks over to the bed, to the magazine. He holds out his hand. Gazing at me, Sally rises and disappears hurriedly into the bathroom. *Is this what life with you is going to be like?*

Sean picks up the magazine, flips through it, prattles on about nothing, high. 'Hot dude,' he says. I hear the shower.

'Take it,' I say. 'It's yours.'

'Oh, but I thought,' he says.

'It's late and you should be in bed,' I say. At the door, I ask him, 'Does your father know?'

It is six o'clock in the morning, the New York sun wrestling through the curtains. In a few hours, Sally and I will make our way out to East Hampton, where I will tell a group of strangers about my son.

'I don't talk to my father,' he says. 'Hey, do you, like, want my beeper number or something?'

After he's gone, I join Sally in the shower. She's pressed up against the wall, the streamers of water indenting the loose ageing flesh of her straight back. 'Tell me, David,' she says, turning toward me, drooping breasts, paunch of a belly, the scar from her Caesarian. 'When did you first kiss a girl? When did you grow hair under your arms? Were you a popular boy? Smart? What did you want to be when you grew up? Tell me who you were.'

I think of Micah. I see him round those orange pylons on his little bicycle. I see him raise his trophy high into the air, the winner's circle. I see him posing on a motorcycle, spread-eagle on the hood of a black Mustang convertible. I see my son's body, his erect penis, the alien glaze in his eyes.

I grab the soap, that tiny bar of institutionalized clean, and lather my body. The smoke leaves my skin; other stains are not so easily lifted. I have neglected whole areas, forgotten the soles of my feet, the back of my neck, sometimes I can hardly touch myself at all.

'I can't keep anything down,' I say, beginning.